I0674519

Calypso's Longing

A Woman's Odyssey of Love

By

Jo Anna Bella
Poet at Heart

A Romantic Novella

Washington DC

Copyright © 2025 by Jo Anna Bennerson

All rights reserved. Except as permitted under U.S. Copyright Act of 1976,
no part of this publication may be reproduced, distributed, or transmitted in
any form or by any means, including photocopying, recording, or other
electronic or mechanical methods, without the prior written permission of
the publisher, except in the case of brief quotations embodied in critical
 reviews and certain other noncommercial uses permitted by copyright law.
For permission requests, write to the publisher, at the e-mail address below.

ISBN: 979-8-9910866-2-2

First Printing 2025

Printed in the United States of America

Published by Luxor Scribe LLC
Luxor_Scribe@yahoo.com

AI Image by Canva

Dedication

For Ilva,
My first diva.

PRELUDE

Calypso's Longing - A Woman's Odyssey of Love

n *this romantic novella, we stumble across the diary of Homer's Greek Mythology Goddess - Calypso, goddess of the tropical island, Ogygia. Calypso, like many of us modern women and men of today, waited for love, experienced love, and lost love only to find that the music of the soul manifests itself through the waves of time: transforming into the rhythm, spirit and carnival of life ~ Calypso ~ even epochs later.*

Following the Trojan War (Homer's Iliad), the great Greek Warrior-King, Odysseus, also known as Ulysses in later Roman mythology - inventor of the Trojan Horse, started his sea journey home to his kingdom of Ithaca. There, his wife Penelope and his son Telemachus loyally awaited his return (Homer's Odyssey), but Odysseus had angered mighty Poseidon, God of the Sea. Poseidon's rage set Odysseus off course and precariously extended his journey home by ten years, following the ten years already spent at Troy during the Trojan War.

After losing all his war treasures, ships, and men and surviving perils like the Cyclops, Circe, the Sirens, sea-monsters Scylla and Charybdis as well as Zeus' wrath because his men had slayed the Sun God Helios' cattle; Odysseus then washed up, battered on a raft, on the shores of Calypso's island. Calypso, unlike many of the other gods and goddesses in Greek Mythology, did not live on Mount Olympus. Rather, Calypso, accompanied by her nymphs, ruled her own realm, Ogygia, an island believed to be in the Mediterranean Sea. In Homer's Odyssey, Odysseus himself praised Calypso saying, 'Calypso of the braided tresses, she took me in, and with all care she cherished me and gave me sustenance'.

Since many of the gods admired heroic Odysseus, they granted him this reprieve in Calypso's paradise where he spent seven years of bliss with her ['The palace of lovely-haired Calypso, though all the time that he was with her he had the comforts a god might have.' – The Odyssey].

Upon returning home, he told the Phaeacians, where he next landed and later told his wife Penelope when he arrived in his homeland of Ithaca, of his admiration and fondness for Calypso. However, the storytellers, Athena & Proteus (within The Odyssey itself) and Homer & Hesiod in their re-telling, persuaded history that mighty, cunning Odysseus had been held captive by this goddess. Hence, she became to be thought of as Calypso, the Concealer; a seductress who diverted a powerful man from reaching his goal; that is, Penelope/Ithaca as the goal versus Calypso/Ogygia as the diversion. Intuitively, we all know that the great king had to return home so that he could tell his story and legend would exclaim his glory. That's how we come to share-in this legendary odyssey.

The Odyssey has become that classic tale of a man not being recognized by his own beloved wife on his return home after overcoming extraordinary obstacles including surviving war, monsters, and unimaginable temptations. Calypso may have been Odysseus' greatest temptation, for she rescued him, offered him immortality and ['the bright goddess, Calypso was joined to Odysseus in sweet love'-Hesiod]. This aspect of the Odyssey allows Odysseus to heal and release himself from the traumas of war before returning to his kingdom of Ithaca. With the earth goddess Calypso's benefaction, it enables Odysseus to choose his future. Ultimately with the Odyssey, the focus of humanity shifts from the immortality and demands of the gods to the will and power of Man himself.

In this romantic, poetic novella of a woman's odyssey of love, in this recently emerged and suddenly discovered private memoire that captures the loving, healing feminine energy embodied by a beautiful earth goddess, in this hidden chronicle of love that embodies the different phases of Love - now these many centuries, later, we hear...HER... her story...through Calypso's varied emotions. Emotions interwoven with contemporary elements transmitting over all times and all spaces, be it the past, present or future, for she inherited foresight from her Titan elders. In this diary, we hear her, her music...we hear the oscillating emotional movements of Calypso!

*IMAGINE STROLLING ALONG THE BEACH,
HAVING THE BRISK ROLLING WAVES SOOTHINGLY CARESS YOUR
ACHING FEET
AND FINDING THERE,
CALYPSO'S DIARY IN AMONGST THE TANGLED WEEDS AND
SUNKED-IN SAND,
ENDURING ITS ODYSSEY FAR FROM THE HIDDEN CAVERNS OF
TIME,
ARRIVING ACROSS THE TELLING AGES INTO YOUR ALLURING
HANDS.*

*...THE SWAYING TIDES EBB AND FLOW,
CHANTING, WHISTLING, MIMICKING...
WHISTLING, MIMICKING, CHANTING, ...
MIMICKING, CHANTING, WHISTLING, ...*

CHANTING, WHISTLING, MIMICKING…

… "HAVEN'T WE ALL BEEN…
…CALYPSO?"

Table of Contents

CHAPTER THREE: THE BATTLE ENSUES
Love Annihilated...A woman suffers Love

CHAPTER FOUR: WEDGED BETWEEN THE GODS, DESTINY AND DREAMS OF PENELOPE
Love Adjudicated... A woman questions Love

CHAPTER FIVE: CALYPSO MUSIC
Love Authenticated...A woman vibrates Love

Calypso's LONGING

L *Longing to capture you. Inside Me.*
Pouring your manhood into my eternity.

O *Oceans of turbulent emotions*
swelling up upon my shores.

N *Native creeks, plunging rivers*
rushing to engulf your sanity.

G *Grasping at your Achilles' tendon,*
hoping to find some cure.

I *Inspired by your burnt,*
sun-drenched skin moistened in my femininity.

N *Nosily suckling your buoyant*
strength through seeps in my core -

G *Gallantly rescuing my stalked heart*
- inside the fort,
- poised for the next victory!

Chart by Jo Anna Bennerson

Greek Mythology

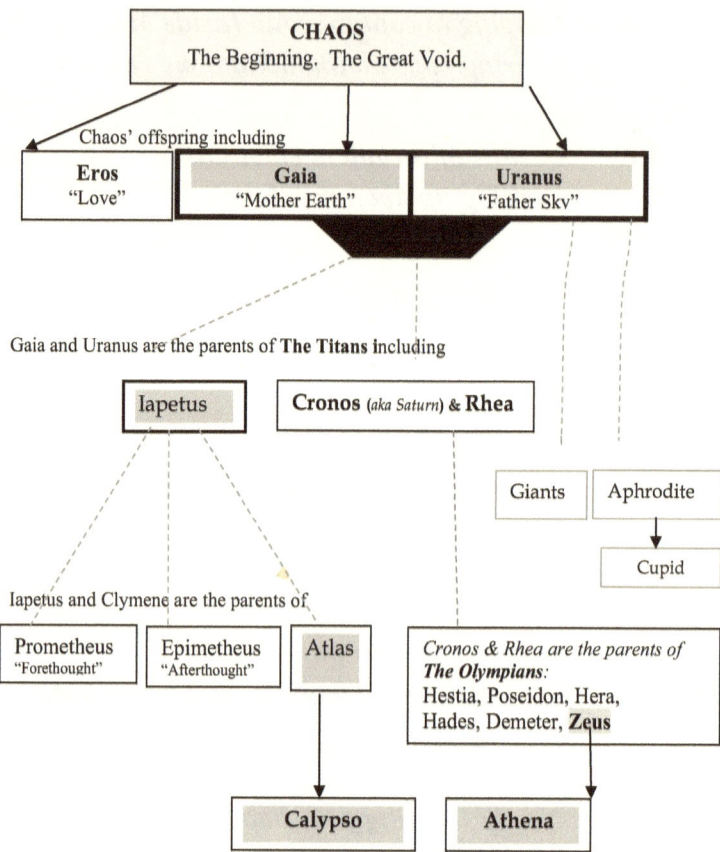

CHAOS
The Beginning. The Great Void.

Chaos' offspring including

Eros
"Love"

Gaia
"Mother Earth"

Uranus
"Father Sky"

Gaia and Uranus are the parents of **The Titans** including

Iapetus

Cronos (*aka Saturn*) **& Rhea**

Giants   Aphrodite

Cupid

Iapetus and Clymene are the parents of

Prometheus
"Forethought"

Epimetheus
"Afterthought"

Atlas

Cronos & Rhea are the parents of
The Olympians:
Hestia, Poseidon, Hera,
Hades, Demeter, **Zeus**

Calypso

Athena

INTRODUCTION

*T*here occasioned a time, when people lived rather intimately with their gods and bigger-than-life heroes, explaining the events upon the earth through well-illustrated stories - tales, myths, legends and shared imagination, handing them down from generation to generation. Such is the gift of Greek Mythology. Its beginning – "Chaos" – the great void produced its first and ever living offspring, "Eros" – Love. Her other descendants are continually revived through the stories (Pandora's Box, the Trojan Horse), terms (Midas Touch, a Herculean effort, Achilles' heel) and words (atlas, the zodiac, nemesis, gigantic) still recited today. Chaos' other children included Father Sky – Uranus, along with Mother Earth – Gaia, who gave birth to many. Among them were the Titans, the youngest being Cronos.

Cronos' sibling, Iapetus and his wife Clymene were the parents of well-known Titans; Atlas – who carried the skies on his shoulders; Menoetius – banished to Tartarus by Zeus; Prometheus "Foresight"- he gave fire to mankind; and Epimetheus "Afterthought" - he married Pandora, who opened the box of miseries that flew into the world; closing it at the last moment, sadly leaving Hope inside. Atlas fathered Calypso, the goddess whose diary we have stumbled upon in this book.

Cronos (later called Saturn by the Romans) led a rebellion against his father Uranus for Uranus despised his children. Just as Cronos led a rebellion against his father Uranus, so did Zeus (known as Jupiter for the Romans) against his father Cronos. Along with his siblings, Hera, Demeter, Hestia, Hades and Poseidon, Zeus waged a ten-year war against Cronos and the Titans who helped him. Zeus, the victor, became the ultimate King of the Gods. He and his siblings, the Olympians who lived on Mt. Olympus, cast the

Titans from the heavens, with many of them descending to Tartarus, bound beneath the earth. Atlas' punishment for fighting against Zeus was to forever bear the sky on his shoulders. His lonely stance was passed on to his lonely daughter, Calypso who lived apart from the gods and the rest of the world on her island Ogygia.

And so it was, throughout the epochs, the constant conquering of lovers, competitors and anything that the Greek Gods fashioned - anything to fill that original and all-encompassing void - Chaos. We find Greek Mythology has chronicled the many lovers of Zeus, Aphrodite and the other gods and the consequences left in their wake. So many were mere pawns in the deities' quest for entertainment.

Consequently, eons later, another great war was beckoned, the Trojan War waged between the Kingdom of Troy and the Kings of Greece. Here, the gods also fought mightily against each other and in support of their earthly favorites. The Trojan War is said to have begun due to the abduction of Helen, 'the face that launched a thousand ships'... that is a thousand Greek ships off to conquer Troy. You will see once you explore more and more of these lusty tales, its origin more likely lies in any number of fragmented routes along the Greek Mythology gamut. For instance, Zeus seduced Leda who gave birth to Helen who was the most beautiful woman in the world; Eris, the Goddess of Discord was not invited to the wedding of Thetis, the mother of Trojan War hero, Achilles, so wedding crashing Eris tossed the golden apple; the three goddesses, Aphrodite, Hera and Athena then vied for the golden apple using shepherd-boy Paris to choose the most beautiful amongst them as Zeus refused to do the judging himself. Paris (soon to be discovered as a prince of Troy) later 'abducted' Helen as she was his promised prize from Aphrodite, the winner of the contest amongst the three goddesses; and on and on. Once this war, the Trojan War ended, its crafty hero Odysseus, a Greek king and the inventor of the Trojan Horse, started his journey home to Ithaca (*The Odyssey*). *Ironically, Odysseus, the mighty trickster had been tricked into participating in the war while trying to trick his way out from having to go to Troy. Thus, when the Trojan War ended, ten years after it had begun, he sought to rush home to this queen and wife Penelope and his son Telemachus who was a baby when he left.*

Odysseus conducts a series of misdeeds, in effect, getting in his own way! These misdeeds offend the gods, even those who may have once favored him, came to be against him; all except Athena. His ego and arrogance brought him into particular disfavor with Poseidon, the God of the Seas. First, he bragged on his victory over Troy, insisting it was because of his cleverness that Greece had won and he refused to give the required burnt offering to the gods. Poseidon set Odysseus' ship off course and then through a series of misadventures. Odysseus upset Poseidon further when on one of these junkets, he blinded Poseidon's son, the Cyclopes - Polyphemus. Finally, he then washed up on Calypso's island - Ogygia. Over time, the gods, except Poseidon, had declared that Odysseus having been the grand human hero who secured Greece's victory over Troy and having endured the sea voyage perils thus far, should have his retreat.

Enjoying all the comforts provided by the Goddess Calypso on her island Ogygia in her spacious, multi-colored marble and limestone metamorphic, refuge cave, with its wide-ranging landscapes, shimmering waterfalls, cascading lakes and mineral infused thermal pools and prancing springs, Odysseus quickly lost touch of time and reality as he indulged in his every fantasy with the goddess. Along with the indulgences afforded him on her island, this diary imagines that they would also whisk away to other times and places, invisible to others, using her magical 'sight' and titan energy; such as future places like the city of Paris and escapades in the Caribbean.

However, Athena, Odysseus' guardian goddess longed

to see him return to Ithaca and pleaded with Zeus to make this happen. Athena was the goddess of war, of crafts, and was known as the Goddess of Wisdom. She had sprung forth from the head of her father Zeus, who swallowed her pregnant mother Methis. Athena is clearly Zeus' favorite. Throughout the telling of <u>The Iliad</u> (the Trojan War) and <u>The Odyssey</u>, it is clear that Odysseus is Athena's favorite.

So, while Poseidon was away visiting the Ethiopians, on the far end of the earth, Hermes, the messenger God, was sent by Zeus to deliver a message to Calypso. The message was that Calypso should let Odysseus go. The mighty accusation that Athena managed to wield against Calypso was that she induced Odysseus with her blandishments. Blandishments are enticements, pleasures not imprisonment! Zeus reminded Athena that it was she, Athena who had requested this reprieve for weary Odysseus. Still, he and the other gods voted that it was time for Odysseus to reclaim his seat in his kingdom. Hence it was decided that generous, welcoming Calypso would have to make this sacrifice of letting Odysseus go.

So, Calypso, despite her loving feelings for Odysseus, obeyed Zeus' command. While upset, she knew better than to tangle with the greater gods, the Olympians, as she was well-aware of their vengeful nature. In her generosity, she graciously sent Odysseus off. Strangely, unlike other Greek gods or goddesses, Calypso did not force her will on her subject but instead invoked free will. We see that in one last attempt to keep the love of her life, she offered him a choice - the gift of immortality; a trait reserved for gods. Odysseus declined. Again, unlike other gods throughout Greek Mythology, Calypso did not enforce her will or punish Odysseus, in fact she helped him further. She took him to a part of her island where he chopped wood to build his raft. She provided food, wine and supplies and even summoned a wind for his sail. It appears as if Calypso's respect for Odysseus represents the gods' newly developed respect for humans. Her generosity, unique among the gods and an emblem of her will, *only adds merit to Odysseus' grandest attribute – having a free will of his own, a will distinct from the desires of the gods.*

One may wonder, why did Odysseus appear, at some point, to be unhappy while there with Calypso? Could it be that this performance was a ploy that Athena employed in order to influence her father, Zeus, to have Odysseus move on to reclaim his throne? It also made for better storytelling by sea-god Proteus and for Homer to tell interesting tales, tales full of conflict in describing this great warrior king as having been detained.

It was quite dramatic to characterize mighty, fearless Odysseus as crying on the shores of Ogygia, yearning to return home to Penelope. Yet one discovers that even on those evenings following Hermes' visit and before his departure, Odysseus willingly made sweet love to Calypso. We also witness that Odysseus had more affairs on his way home to Ithaca after leaving Calypso. For instance, in Scherie with the Phaeacians, where he charms lovely Nausicaa. Apparently, his deep yearning for Penelope does not preclude such encounters!

Today, Calypso's island – Ogygia is not easily found in the Mediterranean. But even back then, with her powerful imagination, with Ogygia bound physically by angry Poseidon, Lord of Earthquakes, we sense that Calypso and Odysseus would whisk away from her island; not visible to human eyes, sailing into other space and time dimensions like the future: voyeurs to distant lands, languages, and eras for their mutual enjoyment. Moreover, as an earth goddess of titian lineage, she was also able to transport her island wherever in various dimensions. Perhaps it's on these magical journeys that she left part of her essence sprinkled on the Caribbean islands where music now bears her name. One wonders about these pleasures, such divine blandishments. Are they why Odysseus could not tell if he was there for one year... three, five or seven years? Possibly nine? Was this loss of time due to all the blandishments, the thrills, the fantasies, he so freely enjoyed?

Calypso's gift of foresight was not unlike others gifted with prophesy, she may have been able to see the futures of others, including Odysseus' but not see her own. Today, with the discovery of this diary, we share in her exploration of love and intimacy. We come to sense and feel that this goddess who was once lonely, who was later vilified by man's "HIS STORY", in fact survived the greatest death of all: love's betrayal and the seeming abandonment of love. But did love vanish?

Through this diary, we will experience a woman's odyssey of love – dreaming of it, discovering it, being hurt by it, questioning it, embracing it. Maybe like Calypso, through her odyssey of love and its different phases, ultimately, we will find ourselves to be happy in the journey that love channels. Might we discover that despite the obstacles, the self-doubt, the abandoning, that Love channels its own energy? Find that Eros is forever more reproducing more waves, more currents, more energy, more frequencies, more love. Can we, like Calypso, love so fully, so deeply, so completely, to release that energy into our universal soul? Channeling songs into a symphony of our own music, music that bears our own name!

Much like Calypso!

Calypso's Diary

AI Image by Canva

As I touch and open this ancient diary

I see and feel

~ A dramatic light show, sounds of cascading waters, mountains, flowers... what a blissful but vibrant scenery.

~ Calypso is a female goddess but can simultaneously form the island mass itself.

~ Her energy fuels furnaces in the rock walls and beneath the island.

~ What amazing crystals, gems, metals and colors brimming with rubies, emeralds, sapphires, gold, silver, diamonds, platinum and so much more – who can name them?

~ This lush island is a showcase of multi-color and clear crystals, cave formations, gems, lush greenery, waves, free running animals.

~ There is a gigantic stance of Titan Atlas overshadowing, which hovers above the earth, his shoulders in a lightly draped silhouette that stands directly above the island,

~ But when his daughter Calypso looks upward, her eyes look upon his face – which no one else sees.

~ See the shape of a shapely woman lying on her side, raised on her elbow on a soft bed, with luxurious drapes and beautiful furniture positioned decoratively.

~ Surrounded by her nymph companions lavishing her with attention - spraying perfume, serving trays of food, she overlooks the island. She chases them off, motioning 'go play'. Her shape even seems to transform into the island mass itself as Calypso senses that a translucent ship-like object is approaching her island inlet.

AI Image by Canva

Chapter ONE

DREAM STATE – AWAITING

Love Anticipated...A woman dreams of Love

And Odysseus answered: ... but as regards your question, there is an island far away in the sea which is called the Ogygian. Here dwells the cunning and powerful goddess Calypso, daughter of Atlas. She lives by herself far from all neighbors, human or divine.

The Odyssey, Book VII

DREAM STATE – AWAITING

Like Pandora, curious to find…Hope,
I arise each morning on my open bay
to the soft blush of a new halcyon day.

Wanting, I scan time's kinescope
from Chaos unto creatures commanding space
racing to find affection ~ attention in my isolated space.

Girl-child of a titan, Atlas - he who holds up the globe,
I drift upon the seas, not on Mt. Olympus, not of Hades.
Alone on a beatific isle, lost in legend, far behind Circe.

Awaiting in my dream state, I goad each horoscope,
I plant passion – fruit to give rise
to your sanctuary; hoping someday…
… to be more than a byline in your story.

AI Image by Canva

Holding this ancient diary
I see and feel...

~ The goddess is moving from working her loom to playing her lyre as she recites fantasy poems "From Eternity" and then moves through various poems to a scene emerging like that of the poem "Vision in the Clouds"

~ Female nymphs are outside of the cave performing chores, with dolphins circling in the circular river that seems like a Minor Oceanus – "MO", surrounding the is.

~ Male sea nymphs in the shape as transparent, luminescent mermen are out beyond the 'MO' circle – serenading the on island female nymphs; splashing into the circle and closer in on the blue waves splashing the islands. As the female nymphs beckon, they come on land, here on land they assume male human form and walk and play with, entertain and assist the nymphs. Are the dolphins shapeshifting? Occasionally, some sirens splashed on by.

~ Wow the circular river (Minor Oceanus – "MO") has rising waterfall streams surging from the ocean into the "MO")

~ As nymphs partner with mermen by day, and disappear at night into the night, we see Calypso alone, in her loneliness, reciting poetry, weaving, sculpting, etc. Calypso's favorite – the dolphins are always dancing and prancing.

~ Ψ – *Trident symbol for Poseidon is seen imprinted on multiple surfaces on the island.*

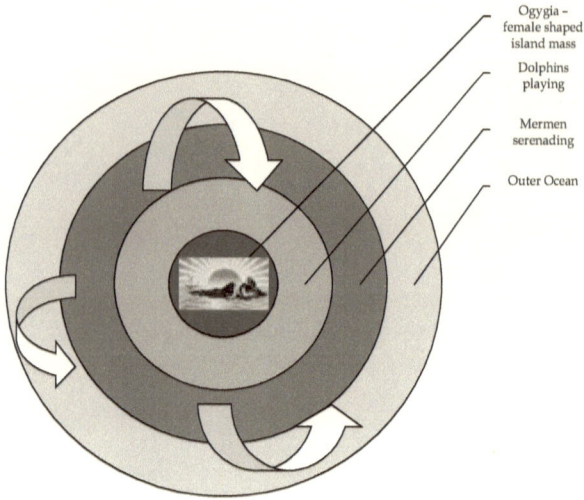

Ogygia – female shaped island mass

Dolphins playing

Mermen serenading

Outer Ocean

From Eternity

From Eternity you emerged through
the veil of the dance, clever verbal pursuits enhanced
the glory of your male form.. *Ah, entranced!*
Tales of Herculean feats, historical places,
romance blooming still in old lovers' eyes
magnify the merger of our two complex mazes
unto the simple treasured road of ulterior highs.

From Eternity, through disguised dreams
from my heart's fortress
you transcend into my reality.

From whence, I pleaded to be amongst the living
I yearned for one, to love, to nurture my spirit.
My first wish did come true
but once on land, the love fell through;
through cracks in the lining
of my family's fighting,
through friends and lovers
conniving and lying.

Thus, did I retreat.
I thanked the Creator for meeting my basic needs.
But resolved that never in this lifetime
would I meet, the one.

The one who existed because I exist.
The one whose touch I dare not resist.
The one who takes all of me and wants more.
The one who gives me himself
until he melts into my core.

From Eternity, though disguised dreams
from my heart's fortress
you transcend into my reality.

Let me honor you, the full expression of "the" you,
the you created by life's ruptures, life's corruptions,
life's nature, life's celebrations.

Let me honor your manhood,
all you stand for, all the centuries you've endured.
Release your manhood, full of hope,
the crises with which you've coped,
the moments when you were at the end of your rope,
all your energy driven deep into concealed isotopes,
into my valley of womanhood.

Find my valley dry but anticipating rain.
Pour down torrential showers upon once fertile plains.
Rejuvenate the vast green inside my femininity.
Produce bountiful harvest to spring upon humanity.

Come forth, no longer retreat.
Plunge through dark forces that block your needs.
For LOVE is the designated sign
that you did meet, the one ... and know

Know that I exist because you exist.
Know that your lips are full to receive my kiss.
Know that my soul has the capacity
to hold your dreams, your former reality,
your fantasies, your new identity.

From Eternity through disguised dreams
from my heart's fortress
you transcend into my reality.

From Eternity, from life's hidden maze,
from Uranus to Pluto, back through the sun's golden rays,
through the parade, march or carnival of this life
into the joy and grief of the everlasting night.

From eternity back to serenity

transcend the space and time continuum,
until WE, you and I, become the total — THE End Sum
of divine creativity,
heralding forevermore our reality, through eternity:

From Eternity.

ONE MOMENT

THERE WE STOOD IN THE CROWD.

TWO COMPLETE STRANGERS; TWO DISTANT
PERSONS.
THE VOLUME OF THE OTHER PEOPLE'S
EXCITEMENT
WAS SO LOUD.
NEVERTHELESS, I STOOD THERE WITHOUT ANY
REASON.

ABSTRACTLY, YOU LOOKED AT ME FROM SO
FAR AWAY
PUZZLED, I GLANCED AT YOU WHEN
GRADUALLY YOU
CAME NEAR.
MY INNER CHILD CRIED OUT,
LET'S RUN OUTSIDE AND PLAY!'

YOUR enthralling GAIT, YOUR ALLURING SCENT
INTERCEPTED MY DIVERSION,
OH, AND YOU LOOKED SO VERY GOOD TO ME.
OUR EYES MET AND SOUGHT something IN
DESPERATION.
WE BOTH KNEW IT WAS love THAT HAD
PROBABLY
BEEN THERE FOR CENTURIES.

THEN WE BOTH LOOKED IN DIFFERENT
DIRECTIONS.
THAT FEELING FOREVER REMAINED IN MY
HEART'S BASEMENT.
WE SHARED AN EXTREMELY PRECIOUS
SENSATION.
WE HAD BOTH EXPERIENCED AND ENJOYED

LOVE for

ONE MOMENT.

My Friend

He did not complain
when I didn't smile.
For he knew
that's not my "Style".
He gave to me
the laughter he had.
Never failed to take away
the tears when I was sad.
He willingly listened to me
and I did the same for thee.
He saw when I looked,
he gave and I took.
A friend, indeed.
One of happiness;
dissolver of misery.
Love is found in beauty,
and my friend in me.

Quand Je Suisse Libre

Avant l'amour, j'ai
declare l'amour dangereux (?)
Avant le voyage.

I WISH I WERE THERE

{For Earl Klugh & George Benson –
from your earth-bound goddess, Calypso
- engulfed in sound, captured by the lure of music,
swaying by on the waves of time}

I wish I were there for your collaboration,
juxtapositioned in your mix, blended into your
groove.
For I would be colorful beyond compare,
free of planetary jinx, tantalized into this
orgasmic mood.
I wouldn't sneeze nor interrupt.
I'd evaporate there in your midst; condensing
the atmosphere.
Transcending known lust,
I'd reach my mystic spot, as you'd recline in
your savor-faire.
*This **is** how I feel hearing your alluring sound.*
I can engulf the scraping magnitude of our
universe.
Like a loaded rocket leaving the ground,
your Collaboration induces this volcanic
outburst!

Destination: Ogygia

Dolphins sailing, Oceanus still
Churning far off to the left.
Baskets full of endless provisions,
Black grapes dripping 'Delights Dionysian'.
Come to her quiet tranquil isle,
Find the terrain wet, no, dry, vast and varying.
Sweet smelling cypress trees await your whiff,
Charming, purified springs anxious for your dip.
Sweet songs emanate from her cave
Luxurious beds and woven tapestries await ashore.
One's ailments, however lethal, sense her cure.
Gold layered currents for sunrises yield
To amethyst draped sunsets, amidst
Turquoise waters so clear, beyond fields
of massive green trees – alder, poplar, all so dear.
'Four running rills of water in channels
Cut pretty close together so as to irrigate the beds of violet
and luscious herbage over which they flowed' and it is so!
'A table loaded with ambrosia',
'mixed him some red nectar'
Be you god or man, you are sure
to enjoy the simply stated splendor.

Even though, an old man,
I still dream of Ogygia, and wish for her,
But it's not to be, all know, I am the time-ravaged Proteus.

Calypso, the nice girl
(Mama Nymph)

'Calypso, the nice girl' is what I call her
She took me into her realm when I was caught in the currents
Them hundreds of years ago
Now they call me Mama Nymph
And I happily help all the others that she takes in
Like Bebe Nymph and the others,
The other lost souls and countless sailors
The human ones, once cured,
When they leave, the memories of Ogygia are devoured
But the other sea creatures often come and go as they please
Them charming mermen linger on the outer edges
Helping us nymphs to live our own heaven
And every now and then, every full moon, in fact
We all dance like banshees in a Dionysian like full moon jam
To relinquish any old sorrows
And to replenish our healing energy here in what he
called the navel of the sea.
Anyhow, Calypso, the nice girl is what I call her
And I pray they'll just let her be.

Besos,
Mama Nymph

Atlas Days

Apollo races his golden charming chariot
across Dawn's still awakening morning.
Wrong side of this family feud sealed my lot,
now flesh, shoulders, back, legs have lost feeling.

How can my mind delight in this new day
that promises new Hercules; heroes?
Free me selfish sky! So heavy you weigh.
Zeus, suffered have I, for your wrath of Cronos.

You marvel in your daughter, Athena.
When shall I embrace mine? True Calypso.
She obeys you Olympians. Shelter,
She is sentenced to provide warring Odysseus. Know!

Know, her beauty resolves my forged weakness
Hold tight! Some day, I partake her caress.

See me, Daddy?

Like a small child, I wait up to hug you.
I doze off, dreaming that you will fly here.
So sad, I'd feel inside, but I'd make do
when jump, skip, hide, go seek...but... you 'not there'.

I blossomed still, free in a tight garden,
sensing your stare protect me from vile vice.
Prayed each night the gods would grant you pardon,
then realized Destiny just twirls blank dice.

Now, a full-grown woman, standing alone
I stretch towards the heavens. Need counsel.
I've come so far but I still need you home.
I have aplenty. Eat, but never full.

Send me your titan mountain terrain strength,
while I go mine love, 'round the river bent.

For Me?
[Dedicated to The Chosen Ones]

Do you mean to tell me
that I am so different,
that the thought of my interacting
amongst you is such an extreme event?

And that my manner
is so not conventional but
unhip nor contemporary
that you know not how to approach me?

Or my accent is so strong
you wonder if it's another language I speak?
That my femininity is so attracting
that the he-male can encounter
only his distracted part of me.

But my independence or need of it
is so commanding that it scares you away?
Oh and that you beware my latent talents for you fear
if allowed to flourish they will surely disrupt your system?

Yes, strangely my reality stems from the ideal.
So easily you claim, there's no room for me to fit.
For so long, the best of me has been concealed.
So of course, I yearn to be a part of "it"!

Indeed, for my composite is so unusual
to you that it even blinds your curiosity
and all you dare to see is a rotating cube
of isolation - designed...just for me?

Vision in the clouds

"Maidens, go play 'pluck the grapes' from the vines.
I'll gather the...what's that?
What is that?   That vision in the sky?"

It's...HE'S LARGE.
Tall, umpteen feet, 3". Shoulders broad.
No forced bulk. Just smooth tight muscles stretched
along lengthy and precisely forged bones.
Masculine, like early men were.
Hail the titans, the gigantes!
But without the ornaments or
other emblems needed to display strength.
No, no
no weighs to bench press -
natural, raw
time-designed by physical law.
True brute force to behold,
so firm, muscular, toned.
Even from this isolated island where I stand
I can tell his force
extends from his telling body to his swelling mind
kinda' sequencing through his vacuous soul.
Is he? Is he the one?
The one not to be taken lightly?
Not one
to just dash in and out, hopping from station to station.
He's made up his mind.
He knows who he is,
here, where in my presence, he wholly exists.

He is the masterpiece and the painter all in one!

He is the vision.
All his magnificence shining through
the dark clouds once covering my noon day sun!

Your Lover

*Shape-shifting Proteus, don't use me once
again,
your favorite person, for your fantasizing.
But I'll do whatever you wish, Apollo
for my wish is yours, radiant sun-god.
So listen intensively, Dionysus, my love.
Let these harmonious vibrations, so well
thought of,
be sent through your most sensitive parts.
For my love is searing, Ares. Strike my heart!
Let us share this happiness now!
Your legend foretells how well you're
endowed.
Make ours different, Eros Exemplar…
…Forget Psyche and let's try….*

THE WORLD'S MOST SATISFYING ART!

The Pajardo African Artifact

It's here! Do it, pleasure me so! No phalanx of warriors is worth your gold.
Transformed from appearing visually nonexistent to baring such evidence to be again sealed non-resistant. I smile, I pray.
I thank the gods for your earthy, earthly existence.

Get the Pajardo, the artifact acquired in adventures off Cape Verde. The exterior appeared small, light, neat, polite, lacked any bragging rights, but something made my senses tingle and I knew I was the earth bound girl to handle it just right. How it banks the rim and fills the hole so tight, I want that Pajardo tonight!

Open the casing!
The long hard wood delights: full, firm, rough yet textured with bronze linings, ah, so smooth, I've got to have my prized African Pajardo tonight.

My friends want me to share this strange delight, and I guess I should. Yea, it pulsates with such awesome might.
Nay, not tonight. I discovered it and it's my treasure, mine, mine, mine!
I've secured this rich pleasure 'til envious midnight, when it shall vanish towards
dense mountains to awaken some other adventurer's respite.

A little Pajardo, every now and then keeps tribes in harmony, united;
keeps tributaries flowing, one-sided; keeps old age safely away, frightened;
keeps major organs vital and some cultured woman knowing. Enlightened ...

...The Pajardo artifact may not be right at hand, but once this treasure is revealed, it does the work of a legion of Hercules-inspired men. This museum piece is not for mere seasonal exhibit nor permanent collection display. No, rather it's a living tribute for which each worthy nymph or goddess prays!

Say it again...Alleluia, Amen, Accolades!

...Ase!

LEAF

Leaf falling
Going down, down, down
Gravity pulling,
So strong, strong.
Wind gliding
Sun is shining.
Force carries
Little leaf along.
There it goes across…
KEEP ON FLYING
…up and down,
Dancing all around.
Um…what,
What happens when the leaf hits the ground?

COMING

*The thought of coming
to your relaxed center, I
play with myself, here.*

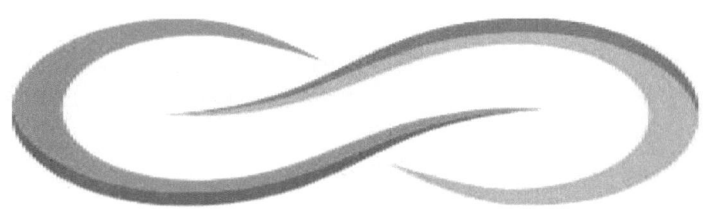

Chapter TWO

Discovering You ~ Finding Me

Love Activated...A woman embraces Love

Fortune, however, brought me to her hearth all desolate and alone, for Zeus struck my ship with his thunderbolts, and broke it up in mid-ocean. My brave comrades were drowned, every man of them, but I stuck to the keel and was carried hither and thither for the space of nine days, till at last during the darkness of the tenth night the gods brought me to the Ogygian island where the great goddess Calypso lives. She took me in and treated me with the utmost kindness.

The Odyssey, Book VII

Discovering You ~ Finding Me

Finding your ocean bruised, shipwrecked, war-torn body
adrift, lifeless on the only jagged edge
of my phantom coast,
I wonder, where along the way, great king
did you lose your esteemed crown,
your coveted royalty?
Why did you catapult
your will against the holder of the realm,
the undisputed king of the seas, volcanic Poseidon?

Discovering you,
here in my private space, drenched,
when not long ago
you went blank in time's crystal ball, whence
you entertained us nightly thru that silly war
and your homebound comedies.
While defined 'goddess',
I'll trump tradition and extend
to you hospitality
and what they'll term humanity,
knowing all the while, that's my in-bred generosity.

Finding me, sunken deeply
in your glazed over, yet adventurous eyes,
I feel a life force I've never experienced before.
Unhurriedly you emerge from that coma induced trance
into your new albedo state of being.
Is it Chi
bringing in my once hesitant,
now eager arms to embrace your being?
Fateful Moirai, oh, I've found my destiny!

Discovering You, Finding Me!

AI Image by Canva

Holding this ancient diary
I see and feel...

~ *Moving through the concentric encapsulating streams protecting Ogygia, Odysseus washes ashore from the ocean.*
~ *Calypso is in a deep slumber induced by Athena, of which the nymphs are unable to awaken her of their discovery. The energy of the island dims lower and lower as Odysseus approaches the island. It then appears to go out when Odysseus starts touching the island (flickering) and then sets to its lowest level when he washes onto the shore.*
~ *Nymphs surround him, wondering if he is "The One" for Calypso.*
~ *When Calypso finally awakens, and visits the shore, she signals the nymphs (now in invisible form so his human eyes can't see) to bring him to the cave. The nymphs summon the neighboring male mermen, who arrive on land, transforming from solid mermen into translucent men and carry Odysseus into the cave to a healing place. 'Others' rescued on the earth and carried here from the turbulent seas are in nearby beds. Calypso summons a separate, royal chamber within as the healing place for this prince amongst men.*
~ *Nymphs singing, rejoicing he's a true human as no other true humans have come*

before, they were all transformed through the atmosphere surrounding Ogygia before they touched the island. Later, when they left, their human forms were returned once in the outer areas of the encapsulating sea.

~ Calypso is smiling that mighty Odysseus is here but lamenting of how she was 'blinded' from his coming, last 'seeing' him at the perilous quandary of Syclla & Charybdis.

~ Odysseus is being pampered, but unconscious with violent reactions as images of his life play out in the shadows.

~ As the island's vibes soothe his body, he imagines a goddess being present, but this seems strange as there is no danger, as with Circe. Odysseus dreams of nymphs holding him.

~ He slowly comes into focus, into reality.

~ Odysseus awakens, sees nymphs, speaks to them, explores the island with them.

~ Calypso presents herself, greets him as the king he is, not the wretched creature that was pulled by the tides onto her shore.

~ As he recovers, a grand sea nymph party with what sounds like modern Calypso music takes place.

~ Jealous old man of the sea Proteus watches angrily offshore.

Healing Vibes

The healing properties of your sacred caves
Drenched in ancient sanctifying natural minerals
Recalibrate my cellular structure.

Anointed lyre strumming healing practices save
Me from drowning in war memories so sinister.
Compelling me to remold my mind, my soul, my posture.

Mental rejuvenation ties with spiritual revitalization
As your sacred prayers, vibrating crystals and physical
therapy
Revive me to rise again, to conceive a new dream, a new
future.

Touched by a goddess, energized by comfort and strength.
Wounded no more, rising from the nightmare of ceaseless
pain.
I now sense it's all you! Your internal healing vibes ~ that's
how I recovered.

Thank you so much Calypso,

Yours,
Odysseus

You are welcome here (song)

You are welcome here
You are welcome here
Lonely, cast away little one

Even in the vastness and cold of this gigantic sea
Here you are welcome and you have a place with me

And the choir of nymphs sing

You are welcome here
You are welcome here
Lonely, cast away, once great one

Even with the vastness and hold of this gigantic sea
Here you are welcome and you have a place to be

And the choir of nymphs sing

You are welcome here
You are welcome here
Found you a spot today to rest in the sun.

Even in the vastness and glow of this gigantic sea
Here you are welcome. Rest, then reboot your journey.

Stand up and emerge into the light

Eyes seeing. Ears hearing. Fingers feeling.
Birds chirping. Deer rustling through the trees.
Is this what it's like to be free?

Beauty in everything. Taste buds climaxing.
Ecosystem palace luxury cave finds me relaxing.
Is this paradise, even real?

Slightly. Don't put pressure oni it.
Look! Feet on the floor. I can stand up by myself.
I'm all the way back from losing me.

Stand up and emerge into the light.
The past is gone. Today is the present.
This moment is my gift, my present – let me be!

Cavern of unique rooms so beautiful

Her home is not one room but multiple
A cavern of unique caves, separate rooms so beautiful
Dazzling stalagmites and stalactites.
Rough/smooth surfaces so enticing that my emotions take
flight.

Some day soon, you'll probably climb in to see
Wonders like I now indulge in but think a dream.
Son Doong's grand chambers seclude mountains
That reach the sky. Here most rooms spring colorful
fountains.

Carlsbad's halls with limestone grace. Nature's artwork in
an ancient place.
Glowworms in a twilight gleam, in a starlit dance forming
flowing dreams.
Mammoth Cave's endless winding trails of labyrinths,
Capri's Blue Grotto currents cascading on the winds.

Colors as vivid as the Reed Flute Cave with purple, blues,
pinks and greens
but only the goddess enters the cordoned off huge Crystals
Cave; left unseen.
So many adventures she has led me to, now, and strange ones
in the future,
From any singular place in this cavern or via her floating
translucent island;
Moments of fantasy that I will always treasure.

Compliment

When it's April, just ever so softly
You hear a murmuring glee as the songbirds sing.
The heavy rain of two days ago becomes a memory as if to
say,
heaven has forgiven all our sins.

So lovely and bright is the day,
The sunshine fills me with tremendous energy.
There's no pollen or dust, like in your cities, to dismay
And my entire realm is too small to confine me.

I stroll across the marble floors to take it in,
To lavish in Hemera's creation of this perfect day.
While in the natural pharmacy as Nana Nymph begins
Her ritual, you happen by my way.

Quick hello followed by a brief conversation
Reinforces this will be a lovely day.
Could this be your message or my imagination
when the reflective limestone walls release your murmurs

"Hey"
"What a pleasant surprise,
What a lovely surprise,
Excellent doesn't even come close,
Gorgeous doesn't even come close.
You just look so beautiful outside
As you are inside, today. Woah".

Oh how poetic you are, how majestic you make me feel.
Your sense of reality need only encompass
The glory of everything outside that's real.
Alas, there's no clever way to say
Your compliment has inspired me today
Like nothing else has.

Just don't touch me, again

Out here, in no man's land I'm more man, more alive on the inside than I've ever been. I've been in every great palace along the coast of Greece. I gorged out outer men's insides. It was like I died inside when I saw princely Achilles die, I went down to scourging Hades and saw my mother cry. I'm a man who has lived to the fullest and had every merriment a king could have and every sorrow a scavenger would ever know. So why is it that here, near you, everything in me rumbles, every rush of the breeze against my chest fills my head not with remorse or foreboding but with other things — with emotions, with dreams, with strong and dense imaginings that materialize so real?

If only you hadn't touched me.

If only you hadn't carried me to safety, if only you hadn't washed my ragged, washed-up body, if only you had not have hand-fed me, and held me in your embrace to impart some of your divine energy. But I'm O.K. now, so please stay, right over there with your maidens. I couldn't take brushing my elbow against your back, again, as it did, when we were out stripping the vines of grapes to make your private-label wine. Picking up the varietals now on the ground, my lips found yours. The sensation that took over me, dam near wreaked me and if it weren't for that spring equinox alder tree, I would have stumbled and fainted like a child dazed by the solar eclipse of the sun.

Please stay way over there, don't come and stand next to me.

You're a goddess, dam it. Flawless. The daughter of a mighty titan. Dam it, your father, Atlas, holds up the skies, so mere humans like me can survive, but you prance around this island paradise like a fawn, rustling through the brushes without a care. Don't you do it, don't glance over here, it feels like a cosmic stare that's piercing through me, lancing through my ligaments and dissecting my body. Stop it, your angelic smile only adds insults to injury. You're so pure, so pleasing to one's sight. Intelligent beyond compare. Confident without being a bore and your spirit knows no fear. Do me a favor, as long as I'm here. Please don't touch me. Kindly, do not stand anywhere next to me. Just don't touch me, again.

Until…until, you do it again.

Only You Knew

You looked beyond my zealous expression
My forever ready smile
You saw the tears I hadn't shed
You heard what I was not saying
You entered that hidden zone
that I dared not reveal.
You were the one who had been able
to see that distant glare in my eyes.
You knew what I had been calling life
was only a game I had been playing
with myself for too long.
Therefore allowing myself to grow
astray
in my world.
You knew I could not
continue keeping "me" a secret.
Extended your arm and held out
your hand, you did.
Filled me with confidence
leading me away from hesitation.
You looked within the depths of my being
 and displayed
my emotions
at the lost and found collection of my soul.
You built me up,
Showed me how to live what I felt.

You listened when I spoke.
You taught me
and well I learned.
How will I ever be able to repay you?

Totally thank you?

Oh Ode D!

Like Me?
I like you!
Kissed me
Oouu! What should I do?

Look at me intensely
I feel it through and through.
Hold me tightly.
Oh Ode D, you know what to do.

So...No! In my cypress heavy park.
OK! I'll just take my abstract art
and move beyond this mirage.
One day, we'll navigate the stars.

And up against my sweet-smelling cypress tree,
The stars did shine, for a few brief eternal hours.
You'll be mine; all mine.

Contemplate? Heck No!
I just know every moment we've spent
is like lost treasure deep in a sun god's cove.
Every rich moment lingers with your male, shucks, man-ness.

Your voice is magical to me
It revs me up and cools me down.
One murmur and I'm ready to please
you up and down, round and round.

Let's make our own heaven on earth, without end.
Let's be, all of everything...loving friends.
Let's feel free to set the tone
of a phenomenon that life itself can't transcend.

You see...Oh Ode D, I like you
and I can feel how you like me. Woo, woo!

And I think what we'll have to do
is keep it new and fun and fresh, real and surreal, too!

In the guise of you

Sorry,
I just needed to feel the brush of your lips
and taste the essence of your tongue.
Selfishly, I longed to thrust my hips
toward your structured torso; so lean, so strong.

I've had you over and over again
in the lusty realms of my sensuous bed.
I envisioned myself – your sexual heroine
but, I could never reveal my dreams unto you. Instead...

...Instead, I think, 'please forgive' my fantasizing about you,
since I know even thoughts are declared dreaded sin.
But know, I felt I had no recourse, once cued
up by the stagger of your muscular, masculine limbs.

It's not your fault, though.
Certainly, I don't blame glorious you.
No, I blame the jealous earth whom I now deeply owe,
for grudgingly unveiling a human so divine,
in the guise of you.

I'm Ready!

I'm ready to hold him tight, to love him with all my might.
True, I've tried and failed; I've sighed AND moaned AND wailed!
So I wanted to give it all up. I wasn't gonna be another lovesick pup.
Yeah, I was real tough. I refused all offers; nothing was good enough.

But as time flew then I finally knew,
that I was rather OK and it was finally my day!
I had been dead; crushed by the weight of love.
Now resurrected, I stand tall - high above.
Above all the maladies and strife, I'm ready to LIVE my life!

Dear Lord, do you hear me? Because of your gifts, I'm ready
to share my life and fantasies with someone who'll love this body.
Love my body, spirit and soul. I'll taste his parts and devour him whole!
'Cause I'm ready to be happy and I'm ready to LOVE somebody!!

Are you ready?

Are you ready
for some loving so mighty
it will tingle your toes
and wet your nightie?

Are you ready
to tremble uncontrollably
when my fingers
tickle places you can't see?

Are you ready
to sweat, cough and wheeze
when sensations inside you erupt,
collapsing your knees?

Are you ready
my big bad wolf
to huff and puff
and never surrender
even when the ecstasy is just too much?

Are you ready?
Send up a signal, throw up a flare
I have so much more for you...
but only if you dare!!!!!!

Love Me Now!

*L*et your heart be free.
*O*pen your pores, so that the stale sweat can come forth.
*V*ary the images that your mind sees,
*E*ase into my arms; forget the hurt.

*M*y feelings may be new, but they're true.
*E*very part of my mind, body, soul craves the essence of you.

*N*o need to be logical, asking when, why, who?
*O*ne more chance, the gods and I have given you.
*W*ill you waste or treasure it? It's up to you!

Fresh Charts!

Falling for you, I'm instantly lifted up!
I'm ravaged by feelings so strong and long overdue,
SPINNING, as lost emotions scramble their way to my tip
top.

The awkward way, I always knew before –
Turns coat – afraid to stand firm before your boxing stance!
Your contemporary designs charge boldly to the closed
door…

…of my once boarded up --///---cordoned off heart.
Somehow with a singular blueprint, you've overwritten
EONS of anguish; forcing LOVE to draft us fresh charts!

Act: YES

How is it that I feel this way?
I thought we'd just meet on the Aegean bay
for the sake of it,
departing with the usual dismay.
But the Fates decided to halt that routine
and now I'm sure that I'm in love,
in this role of life; Act YES: the first scene.
It thrills me so.
The feelings running through my being-
the joys of your usurping my soul.
Who are you, human hero, to ask me out?
To walk and talk, wine and dine, kiss and hug;
making my nerves leap, twist and shout?
Only the power of Fate
could let me be uncontrollably happy,
even as my insides shake.
So now,
I yearn to see you yet again.
To have you captivate me as I indulge
in your desire for me.
The way of the first encounter,
the way we did, trembling, over and over, then.

ACT...yes, Yes, YES!

Go ahead goddess girl. Work your thing on me!
(Chamber Door!)

Go ahead, Calypso, Miss Oh So Fine,
You've invited me into the 'guest' part of your secret realm.
And I must say, your red, red wine competes for
deliciousness
with your island breeze, your sweet singing and how you
seem to make time fly.
So that's all good ...but it's time...
alright, miss goddess girl, let's see what you have in store.
I have a Greek queen back home, I had Trojan maidens
galore,
I had 'sexy as hell' Circe seduce me and turn my men into
pigs and boars.
What can you do? Besides nurse, feed and entertain me?
It's time you let me make you scream and shout til your
vibrations make your
daddy Atlas shake and drop the world off his shoulders onto
the ocean floors.

Open that chamber door!

You say such stunning things, cunning Odysseus, mighty
warrior king.
I am pleased to share my hospitality with such royal nobility
but please don't think me a whore. Sleeping with wayward
immoral, mortal men is just not my thing!
Like any woman - goddess or Pandora-bred
I want my own man, my own true love, a soulmate to love
outright,
not only to sex in the dark, or in a cave, but deeply adore,
everywhere, in any form, any kingdom or in any day or
moonlight.

Sorry, but I can't open the inner vestiges of my PRIVATE
chamber door!

Miss Calypso, you know, you want me. I see how you look at
me
and that's not pity. After being shipwrecked, thanks to you
and your crew,
I'm now fully restored, and I mean in every possible way.
I've never had a woman deny me, I mean, who, on earth
could say no!
And a woman who has been as alone and lonely like you,
you want me, don't you? Just admit you do. I can tell! You
make sure
you lock yourself in your chamber, long before the day is
done.
Is that your way to deny yourself, this bundle of manly
pleasure, to say 'no-no' to fun?

Girl, fling open that boarded up, locked down chamber door!

Ode D, you speak like no other man, your words are
entertaining and that aspect I like,
but don't get it twisted, your dam near divine body ain't
enough
to make me lose my everlasting, goddess mind. Boy, let's not
fight!
True, your sexiness is paramount and your style cleverly runs
from smooth to rough
and that makes any woman almost ready to un-shield her
body's defense,
but I've got some sense. I know Athena is your private deity,
I know your wife Penelope awaits your return eagerly,
don't use your newfound strength to lay me down.
You better make some rounds, bout this island to build
yourself a raft
so you can take your sexy hard core home. The gods didn't
grant
you refuge to my home just so you could score!

**You better stop sniffing up under my cherry scented,
well defended chamber door!**

Calypso, you can say what you want, but I won't leave you alone' til
you share in the wealthy treasures of me. It's the least I could do to repay your hospitality!
Don't you worry about Athena or Penelope, I know how to handle them.
What are you afraid of, that someone will learn of our intimacy?
I promise you right here and now, no one will ever say you kept me,
that somehow your sexiness or goddess powers detained me.
I'm Odysseus, DAM IT! All know I'm free and because of my will and cleverness,
I survive and no one, no one could ever trap me!
So stop being a frightened little girl, and be the woman I dream of every summer night.
Let me make this incredu-lust love to you, goddess-girl, I'll rearrange your history!

I grant you permission goddess-girl, to work your thing on me!

That's right, goddess-girl, find the key, wiggle with the lock, pretend you're going right
to sleep...un hum...crack open that chamber door...just a little bit! Give yourself to me.

Jouez!

Jouez avec moi!
Il pleut mais nous avons chaud!
Entres dans ma chambre.

WORLDWIDE

I stretch my love wide,
You descend upon my thighs.
The earth shakes, I sigh.

Rain Anew

Rain
Gray skies shed impervious lights.
Pain
washes away, by the fortnight.

Seven sudden inches of unheralded pleasure
launched in my deserted soil.
I cry out praises of thanksgiving,
so long, I've toiled.

The harvest is already dead.
Still, the earth remains.
Rain
leaves whims of joy, heartache;
replenished hope, seasons anew – life stained.

Rain

I yearn ever more deeply for rain.

How I wish I were a painter.
{by Calypso & Odysseus}

Both:
How I wish I were a painter
so that I could draw out the rich tones, hues of your skin.

Odysseus:
I wish to dab my brush in moist damp paints,
etching through your veil of finely woven limbs.

Calypso:
I'd arrange all comforts for your enduring statuesque pose...

Odysseus:
...charming you with the rapid, fluid strokes of my brush.

Odysseus:
I'd drape you in confidence with my "j'adore" filled smile...
   ...knowing just when to look away;
   if my eyes were saying too much.

Calypso:
I'd caution you not to move so much as an inch
so that your form forever mounted,
could frame my still life...

Odysseus
...and when you would pout, fuss and argue,
I'd dangle you on canvas, suspended from pinnacle heights.

Odysseus:
You'd stare at me, curious just how much of you I saw.
You'd get edgy and uptight, that, I was getting through;
through all your years of fences and defensive built up.
You'd plot to get more weapons –
the new biological brew.

Calypso:
You'd tremble not from the chill wafting through the air
'stead from my sculpture's emerging form,
cast in my brilliant style.
You'd gasp toward the end, to see yourself look
so divine in my eyes,
standing frozen in time,
finally... speechless for a while.

Odysseus:
Your leaking expression would query how
a mere mortal_could dare assign such profound godliness
and majesty to your image.

Calypso:
Your unwinding nerves would make you shiver all over,
making me feel I'd well-earned my wage.
By the way, what is it?

Calypso:
I'd tell you I painted you so regal but yet so free
for I'd selflessly recognized the god in you.

Both:
I'd explain how you represented heaven and earth to me,
because your character and strength were found in so few.

Odysseus:
How I wish I were a painter
so I could model you in the simple nude.

Odysseus:
So I could inject your arteries, veins, fingers,

Both:
your heart - with my emotions, my lust, my moods.

Calypso:
How I wish I were a painter
then I could bind a pedestal to your matted and
framed work of art.

Both:
Then I could forever keep your glorious reflection
exhibited in my private collection,
next to my dripping heart.

ULYSSES' CANDY

EVERY TIME YOU OPEN ONE LITTLE CANDY,
THINK OF SEDUCTIVELY UNWRAPPING ME.

EACH TIME YOU PUT ONE IN YOUR MOUTH,
THINK OF ALL THE JOYS DOWN SOUTH

WHEN YOU LICK YOUR LIPS...OH SO SWEET
THINK OF HOW GLORIOUS IT'S GONNA BE.

AND WHEN YOU SUCK THE JUICES OUT,
FANTASIZE ABOUT THE WONDERS OF MY MOUTH.

NOW, IF YOU'RE BECOMING A LITTLE HOT IN YOUR
SEAT,
THAT'S EXACTLY WHAT YOU'VE DONE TO ME!

HONEY, NECTAR, AMBROSIA---I'D CALL THE FLAVOR
OF ME.
I REALLY WANT YOU TO LIKE IT, ULYSSES...
...IT'S YOUR CANDY.

For the SEX of it

I want to push my hand up
beneath your white starched shirt,
with red corporate tie hanging.
To excite the warmth of your skin,
as my mind wobbles in sin,
to climb to the apex of your left nipple,
to pull it, pinch it, and dream of licking it.
Just for the sex of it.

I long to ask you, to remain seated
in your drivers seat, with yours knees spread,
parting abruptly at the curve of the wheel...
ask if you could please expose your member so I could feel
you up, or devour your long salami as a meal.
I won't bite. Sorry...just nibble, gobble
and suck, and swallow hard; consuming it.
Just for the sex of it.

With desire engulfing me,
penetrating every curve and crevice on my tortured body,
I shut my eyes. There I see you shoving my
left leg forcefully away from my right thigh,
your fingers march front and center as I sigh.
The little man in the boat is suddenly a rebel,
paddling strong and hard before the storm hits.
Just for the sex of it.

Is this deja vu or am I reminiscing?
Were you moaning, wheezing, or singing
when you freed my two inmates from their cage?
Promptly training them to dance on stage,
opening up, fully exposing all penned up rage.
Now whenever they see you
they contort into a convulsive fit,
Just for the sex of it.

Did your muscles just cram up from a spasm?
Did that white musky fluid result from an orgasm?
Why must you always flush and drain
every single molecule up through the main,
rocking and screaming as you writhe in pain?
Oh, it's pleasure when you come to such a release?
Alright, then it's good you didn't blank out and quit.
I mean, just for the sex of it.

Sanctuary

I roam high vast stacks,
researching your library.
Speechless. Still reading.

In a Dream State of Being

I lived so long to get to NOW

*You, the dream, have become a vision reflecting off
my mirror.
You encapsulate a cherished never before sniffed
scent.
You were the quotient of my calculated long division.
You have become all the things of which I'd
reminiscence.
How could that be?*

~I lived so long to get to NOW~

*I'd reminiscence sensuous moments never having had
any.
Was I just another lovesick goddess?
Could there reveal a day of Love for the
dream-weary?
Yet here you are in the flesh, ready for harvest.
How can this be?*

~I lived so long to get to NOW~

*You pour out love, I drink you in.
You play the lyre. I dance on the wind.
Your smile causes me to climax inside.
You come over me and now I exist in reality ...*

*...I am!
We are!
Realized, that's me.
Now...I BE!*

In a state of Being because of the dream
~I lived so long to get to NOW~

You see me.
You feel me.
It's real.
I BE!

In a state of Being
~I lived so long to get to NOW~

Forever Yours, Forever Mine
A Wedding Song

With God's blessings and in his glory
my life is yours: for you are my story.
Our children will be born into our glow,
truly adopted into what our friends know
is the eternal love and respect I have for you.
In your eyes lies the whole wide world, exciting and new!

Forever yours, Forever mine.

I want to walk over every trail,
sail every sea and every ocean.
I want to visit every distant land,
to experience every sound and every motion!

Forever yours, Forever mine.

I want to explore every region of this man's earth.
Because of you,
I discovered myself and finally know my worth.
Destiny demanded that you and I meet
and so we'll travel together throughout time...
Forever; forever yours, forever mine.

With God's blessings and in his glory
my life is yours: for you are my story.

I'll nurse your hurts, you'll attend to my wounds...
your loving touch could never come too soon.
We'll share our future plans and all our dreams,
Together we'll beat any Olympic team.

Forever yours, Forever mine.

Several times we've tried; not once did my love die.

You're so unique, you're the apple of my eye.
Let's travel together throughout time
Forever; forever yours, forever mine.

Forever yours, Forever mine.

Destiny demanded that you and I meet,
now EVERYDAY is a special treat,
as we travel together throughout time.
Forever; forever yours, forever mine.

With God's blessings and in his glory
my life is yours: for you are my story.
Our honeymoon will celebrate,
our love; as our wedding will dissipate
any fears we have about family and trust;
for marriage and trust form the bridge between love and lust.
My only lust is to enjoy EVERYDAY in EVERY WAY
with you, my love. With you I'll always stay.

Never have our feelings been so intense,
The difference now is there is NO pretense.
We're free to be ourselves in each other's presence:
This is life, this is life's ESSENCE.

I loved you before, I love more now.
I never thought our love could grow...I mean...how?

Rising

The moon
>   lowers
>   her lucid self beneath the sneaky horizon.

Sun,
>   Amen Ra
>   rises slowly, gloomily, trying selfishly to hide
>   his golden color.

Morning
>   Pretty girl Dawn peaks out restlessly,
>   Blinking nervously.

Sky,
>   filled with laughter, boundless color.
>   It's T-O-D-A-Y – Finally!

Da-dum!

Love,
>   reverberating Eros,
>   is Everywhere To Be Seen!

Our Destiny

*Discovering you
snubs oracles, prophesies.
Finding me – ordained!*

Chapter THREE
The Battle Ensues

Love Annihilated...A woman suffers Love

(Athena pleading to Zeus.)
*"But my heart breaks for Odysseus, that seasoned veteran
cursed by fate so long – far from his loved ones still, he
suffers torments off on a wave-washed island rising at the
center of the seas. ...Atlas' daughter it is who holds
Odysseus captive, luckless man – despite his tears, forever
trying to spellbind his heart with suave, seductive words and
wipe all thought of Ithaca from his mind."*

The Odyssey, Book I

(Calypso to Messenger God Hermes)
*"God of the golden wand, why have you come? A beloved,
honored friend, but it's been so long, your visits much too
rare. Tell me what's on your mind. I'm eager to do it,
whatever I can do...whatever can be done."*
*And the goddess drew a table up beside him, heaped with
ambrosia, mixed him deep-red nectar. Hermes the guide
and giant-killer ate and drank."*

The Odyssey, Book V

The Battle Ensues

Love is desired. Is it not?
Companionship is the goal, right?
So what's this twisted plot?
What's this twisted plot?
I can't make heads or tails of it.
Maybe you can fill me in, mister warrior
autobot.

Autobot? Yes, apparently something is
pulling your strings
Or winding your wheels or grinding your
heels.
It matters not! Our love boat has collapsed
and is sinking.
Love domination is said to be a thing
Either you rule me or I run you.
It's never even!
And so the battle ensues. Like you said
"Fuck, my feelings"!

AI Image by Canva

Holding this ancient diary
I see and feel...

~ *Athena has pleaded with King of the Gods,*
Zeus to have Odysseus leave and go
home to Ithaca.
~ *Hermes is sent to deliver the message to*
Calypso.
~ *Meanwhile, Odysseus has been seen crying*
on the shores of Ogygia as Calypso
senses that Athena has summoned this
for dramatic effect to her plea.
~ *After Hermes's visit, the sunny fun filled*
days have passed, replaced by a lurking
deep sadness across the island and
surrounding waters.

~ **Quote from The Odyssey, Book 5-**
After Athena's plead to Zeus, Zeus sends
Hermes to Ogygia
"You are our messenger, Hermes, sent
on all our missions. Announce to the
nymph with lovely braids our fixed
decree: Odysseus journeys home – the
exile must return.
But not in the convoy of the gods or
mortal men.
No, on a lashed, makeshift raft and
wrung with pains,

*on the twentieth day he will make his
landfall, fertile Scheria, the land of
Phaeacians, close kin to the gods
themselves, who with all their hearts
will prize him like a god and send him
off in a ship to his own beloved land,
giving him bronze and hoards of gold
and robes –
more plunder than he could ever have
won from Troy if Odysseus had
returned intact with his fair share.
So his destiny ordains. He shall see his
loved ones,reach his high-roofed house,
his native land at last"*

**~ Quote from The Odyssey, Book 5-
Hermes, the Messenger God is astounded by
the beauty of Calypso's island paradise home**
*"Why, even a deathless god
who came upon that place would gaze
in wonder,
heart entranced with pleasure. Hermes
the guide,
the mighty giant-killer, stood there,
spellbound."*

**~ Quote from The Odyssey, Book 5-
Hermes visits Calypso to deliver the news
from Zeus that Odysseus must leave.**

*"A great fire blazed on the hearth and
the smell of cedar cleanly split and
sweet wood burning bright*

*wafted a cloud of fragrance down the
island
Deep inside she sang, the goddess
Calypso, lifting
her breathtaking voice as she glided
back and forth
before her loom, her golden shuttle
weaving.
Thick, luxuriant woods grew round the
cave,
alders and black poplars, pungent
cypress too,
and there birds roosted, folding their
long wings,
owls and hawks and the spread-beaked
ravens of the sea,
black skimmers who make their living
off the waves.
And round the mouth of the cavern
trailed a vine
laden with clusters, bursting with ripe
grapes.
Four springs in a row, bubbling clear
and cold,
running side-by-side, took channels left
and right.
Soft meadows spreading round were
starred with violets, lush with beds of
parsley."*

AMBUSH

Parties entwined,
Maneuvering together through space and time.
At once a bloc,
Suddenly separate factions; emotionally interlocked.
One – naive, tolerant, unsuspecting.
The other – defiant, scheming, unrelenting.
Seemingly engaged in standard operations,
Truly distant; connected only on brief occasions.
The acquiescent yearning for interaction,
Seeks amusement through a novice association.
There, only to be 'caught'
Causing the suspicious ally much distraught.
Accusations of neglect denied.
Allegations of distrust implied.
"When were violated –left alone?"
"Where on earth were you? Surely not home."
Cunning machinations convince the 'unsuspect'
that all is restored with no loss of respect.

The honeymoon is consummated with much passion;
so intense.
The participants ascend to a new level of relation:
no pretense.
In the delicate moments of feverish afterglow,
All weapons (stockpiled) are left to lay low
Never before so vulnerable, so exposed,
Much like man and woman in the hills, stripped of clothes.
Except it is a hungry lion yanking the very throat
Of the guileless fawn with whom he just asserted an oath.
Rage and terror portray harbored emotions.
Struggle and will struggle against complete domination.
Once set out on a clearing on a clear summer night.
Seduced by tokens of affection, pleasing to one's sight.
JOLTED! Bombarded by rockets, pierced by arrows,
Infiltrated by millions; seeing no tomorrow.
Ambushed by friend...not foe.

Abandoned long ago by LOVE; our fallen hero.
Ambushed; lying on the plains mangled.
TAKEN DOWN,
Shot from every angle.

DESIRE - THE BATTLECRY

*FOLLOWING YOU AROUND, SNIFFING YOU OUT LIKE
HUNTED PREY,
YOUR WANTON SEX AND FEROCIOUS PANTINGS
MAKES ME CRAVE
YOU*

*LIKE
MIGHTY ZEUS PINED FOR PROMETHEUS' NOVICE
CREATIONS
LIKE
HITLER HUNGERED TO SUCK THE VEINS OF EACH
NATION
LIKE
COMMANDER IN CHIEF WHAT'S HIS NAME HELD IN
HIS VEXATION
LIKE
BOYS HOLD ON TO THEIR FIRST DISCOVERED
ERECTIONS.*

*DETERMINED TO HAVE YOU DESIRE THE QUENCH OF
ME -
DRINKING FROM EVERY BRANCH, LICKING EVERY
STEM OF MY CHERRY TREE
UNTIL*

*YOU SPUN OUT OF CONTROL AND SCREAMED OUT
FOR VENGENCE
UNTIL
YOU DUTIFULLY MASSAGED MY FEMININE CURVED
BACK OUT OF TENSION
UNTIL
YOU KNELT IN FRONT OF ME, PLEADING TO ATTEND
MY CORONATION,
UNTIL
YOU SUBMITTED; YOUR ENTITY WAS VOID OF ANY*

INTELLIGENCE.

YOU LIE THERE HOPING TO ACHIEVE SOME
BALANCE,
CONSPIRING WITH YOUR LOST MIND TO ESCAPE
IRRELEVANCE,
AS YOU HAVE BEEN

CASKED INTO THE TRANQUIL EYE OF MY AFRICAN
HURRICANE
 YOU'VE BEEN
STRIPPED OF YOUR RIGHTS, YOUR POWER, YOUR
AEGEAN NAME
YOU'VE BEEN
SHACKLED IN MY BED, AS I AND THE WORLD
CARRIED ON THE SAME.
YOU'VE BEEN
CARELESS IN YOUR DOMINATION OF ME. HA! NADA
IS YOUR GAIN!

YOU STRODE UP... BOLD AND COCKY IN YOUR SMOKY
DARK SKIN.
YOU CARESSED MY BREAST THROUGH SMOLDERING
EYES DRENCHED IN SIN,
DARING ME

TO SEE YOU IF YOU CALLED, LATER TO QUESTION
MYSELF IF I HAD ANY VIRTUE AT ALL.
DARING ME
TO TAKE OFF MY UNDIES, IN THE FRONT SEAT OF
THE CAR, ON THE CROWDED BOULEVARD
DARING ME
TO TELL YOU MY NAKED FANTASIES IN THE MIDDLE
OF THE MALL
THEN DARING ME
TO RECOVER MY SENSES FROM LAST NIGHT WHILE

YOU GO TO PLAY BALL.
NOW YOU LIMP AROUND BROKEN OF HEART.
TRUTH IS – YOUR SPIRIT, YOUR MIND, YOUR BACK
ARE ALL PULLED APART.
BECAUSE

YOU CHARGED IN AND SAVAGELY STOAKED MY
SEXUAL FIRE.
BECAUSE
YOU HURRIEDLY AND WITH TOTAL DISREGARD
REVVED UP MY CARNAL DESIRES.
BECAUSE
YOU WOULD NOT YIELD, EVEN AS I LAY NUMB. BOY,
"I'M JUST TOO TIRED."
BECAUSE
YOU MADE ME YOUR ADDICT; SCARY, SCARED,
STRUNG OUT AND WIRED.

DAMMED BY THE CURSE OF THE JEALOUS FURIES
TO PROCURE YOUR HEDONISTIC PLEASURES OR
SUFFOCATE IN MISERY,

I TURNED
INTO THE ORPHIC ASHES RISING TO YOUR EGYPTIAN
PHOENIX.
TURNED
INTO YOUR EXPOSED ACHILLES HEEL - SUBJECT TO
EVERY TOXIC STICK.
TURNED
INTO THE WHIPPING POST OF YOUR EPICUREAN
CRUCIFIX
TURNED
INTO YOUR DANCEHALL MUSE, CHANTING THE
PRAISE OF AN INSATIABLE LUNATIC.

SO I HAD TO SURVIVE, AND I WOULD SUCCEED
TO WITHSTAND YOUR MADDENI NG CONSUMPTION,
YOUR SENSELESS DESIRE, YOUR RAVENOUS NEED.

*I CONTROLLED
WHETHER YOU CLIMAXED, CRASHED OR CAME.
I CONTROLLED
WHEN THE THUNDER AND LIGHTNING CAME WITH
THE RAIN.
I CONTROLLED
IF YOU COULD GO OUT OR JUST SIT UP UNDER MY
WINDOW FRAME
I CONTROLLED
IF YOUR MANHOOD COULD BLUSH OR WINK FOR
SOME OTHER JANE.*

*YOU, DARLING, OPENED THE CORRODED
FLOODGATE.
NOW, I'M YOUR SEXUAL DRIVER. DON'T MAKE ME
WAIT!!!*

*BE THERE
WHEN I WANT YOUR BRUISED LIPS BRUSHED ACROSS
MY BERING STRAIT.
BE THERE
WHEN I DEMAND YOU SNORKEL IN THE CLOUDY
WATERS OF MY WINTER LAKE.
BE THERE
IN THE MORNING WHEN I WANT A 6.5 EARTHQUAKE
ON THE RICHTER SCALE.
BE THERE
CERBERUS, SOP IT UP! LIKE THE DOG YOU ARE,
AFRAID, EVEN IN HADES, TO WANDER AWAY!*

IF SHE, PENELOPE

If she woke up
From her deep slumber,
You'd be there, Prince Charming
Waiting and smiling, happy to grant her welcome.

You're still in love with her.
Even after these many years
Of being a bank account, a lost hero, a distinct blur.
All to drown inside your own pool of tears.

You're hoping, wishing on your knees praying
She'll forgive you some past transgression.
You're spending, you're travelling, you're playing
Sports to create a diversion.

You meet me and I make you happy.
You clearly know, I make you glow.
Yes, I know of your devotion to your family.
I just wonder why you don't understand, she thinks, "So?"

(It's not about me!)

If she throws you a bone
Even a splintered, ragged, dog pound reject.
You'd roll over and run on home
Allowing your fantasies to fix the defects.

If only she looked ever so slightly in your direction,
You'd spin cartwheels, do handstands
You'd bend, kneel or take any position
The queen set forth in her royal land.

You see you're a mistreated
Lonely being of a man
And even when it was me you overheated,
You just can't help being "Mrs. THING's Husband.

Stand up now, be a man!
You've tried, everything, everything you can.
Now do something for yourself, make a plan.
'Cause being loyal doesn't mean being a
_____ husband.

(fill in the blank)

Diffused
Mis-used
Confused
"You L-o-o-s-e-d"
Mentally Abused
"Pay your dues"
Sing the blues
Emotionally battered and bruised

"Dare to lose your cool"
"Boy, you're a fool"
"Just pick up the kids for school!"

Don't take my love for granted

You know, I'm here for you
So you act reckless with the things you do.
You go out all hours of the night.
You know better, it just ain't right.

Don't take my love for granted

I nurse you when you're sick
I kiss places no one would lick.
You forget, I do these things because I want to,
You strut around saying, "I have to."

Don't take my love for granted

Maybe it's true, I'll always love you
But I won't spend the rest of my life
Going through hoops for you.
Take a long good look at me,
Decide right now! ... if you want me.

Don't take my love for granted

If you want me for all eternity
Treat me right and then you'll see
Even much more of the love,
I started to hide deep inside of me.

Don't take my love for granted.

You've Sown Your Seed

Here I am
Awaiting your arrival.
Am I insane?

Why do I
Need you for my survival?
Am I just another stupid Jane?

I actually feel
So concerned and lonely
when you're not here.

Yet, I'm so stimulated
By your interest and sense of
Reality, whenever you're near.

I don't know
If it is love I feel,
But you I certainly need.

All my infirmities
You alone have healed.
Yes, you've certainly sown your seed.

Restez!

Restez, s'il vous plait.
Je me sens pas bien.
Quand est ce que vous retournez?

I Know We're Just Lovers

I know we're just lovers
but next time, can we make love?
I know we just hit it
but they're other sensations I'm thinking of.

Just because we meet at night
don't mean we can't magnify/delight our souls.
Just because we're Eros lovers
don't mean we can't reach a higher plateau.

Let me knead your massive shoulders,
rub down your aching head, swirl my fingertips through
your dangled hair.
Yes. Take my face in your tailored hands,
swing your mighty arm around my tush. You'll find peace
there.

Sit here in my easy chair; dangle your feet in the cool blue
tub,
shake off the funk of the crumbling street.
Wait! I'll do it, I'll massage your feet. I'll scrub.
Relax, set your back at ease.
Let me lay my head in your lap...PLEASE?

The stale potpourri hangs in the midnight air.
You've brought Italian wine and Egyptian beer to wash away
our cares.
Linger here in my bed tonight,
let me inhale your sanguine fragrance till the morning light
know we're just lovers
but next time, can we make love?
I know we said we'd just hit it
but they're other dimensions I'm thinking of.

Shall we go to Ocean City and frolic on the boardwalk?
Pass through that narrow alley, while we laugh and talk?
Talk to me. Speak to me the blustery inlets of your heart.
Whisper from within, the far-flung dreams on your pushcart.

Trip me up on the hotel room's carpet.
Bruise my knees on the fireplace's parapet.
Lick my juicy lips with your full, pronounced growth.
Explode in me, again and again, without remorse.

Close your eyes. Trust me. Lie quietly on your belly.
Stretch your spectacular arms out above your head.
Lie still,
as I tie you by scarf to my anxious bed.

Is it a feather, an artist's brush or my writing pen?
Did I sketch a woman's LA LA or Ares' foreskin?
Do you like the heat rising from your dark skin,
from this lotion that blows hotter that the south sea winds?
I know we're just lovers
but this time, can we make love?
I know we agreed to just hit it
but they're other commotions I'm thinking of.

No. I won't invite my girlfriend over to join in,
just like you don't want to see another man straddling me.
Perhaps, we can compromise and fast forward to Caligula'
Rome,
sit in a back room; vicariously enjoying an orgy.

Ah, ooh, cool strips of ribbon soaked in adolescent
Manischewitz
hang over my limber limbs like a celestial virgin.
Abruptly, your creativity emerges!
Whew! Devour this sacrifice. Zeus, I pledge my allegiance!

Reach into your pants and relieve your stress.
Go on, I dare ya, make a mess on my pretty blue dress.
Comb through the thick brush on my mountain terrain,
wash down my valley with your saliva or your tears.

Drench me in your overpriced cologne,
cloak me in your Armani suit, just in -
flown from Paris. Sniff my lacy lingerie,
as you caress my universal tenderness.

I know we're just lovers
but this time, shall we make love?
I know we thought we'd just hit it
but they're other creations I'm thinking of.

Blow me a kiss from across the crowded market aisle.
Wink at me, handsome! Greet me with a smile.
Tug my elbow, squeeze my waist, close your eyes,
call out my name, lustfully, all the while.

Call me in the afternoon, let me ask you "why?".
Have me giggle that you've named the region in-between my
thighs.

Trace the roaming lines in my once nervous palm.
Enter the cavern. Are you scared because it's calm?
Excite me then! Use your mind.
Tell me a story of how you hunted, seized, and consumed
your prey.
Show me how you performed on that first meritorious day.

Cry in my pillow because you've loved and lost.
Demand you shalln't be that vulnerable again...at any cost!
Valiantly, I mount my mare above your triumphant torso.
Ergo! You burst into my Trojan horse at full strength and
manly force.

I know we're just lovers
but it's delectable to make love.
If we keep it intimate, we can always hit it
'cause they're so many scenarios to think of.

The Secrets to Romancing…The Great Ode!

The Secrets to Romancing…The Great Ode!
The Secrets to Romancing…The Great Ode!
The Secrets to Romancing…The Great Ode!

Sirens, you thought I'd hear
your message and disappear.
You talked to me rough and caused many tears.

I'M SO SENSITIVE, TRUSTING, AND LONELY…POOR,
POOR ODE!

Calypso, you detected my little
flashes of seeming intellect.
You surpassed my concubines and wife
with your steamy island sex.

THE POOR MARRIED, YET ROAMING FREE, HORNY,
GREAT ODE!

That witch Circe didn't like the way
I talked my macho talk.
So she desperately kicked me to the curb
in the cold, Hades-bound, lonely dark.

BUT CALYPSO, WOULD YOU DO THAT TO YOUR
SWEETHEART?
THE SWEET, CUNNING, DEBONAIR MAJESTIC CAPTAIN
ODE!

But I re-emerge again and again,
'cause, Nausicaa, I want you all to be my girlfriends!
And women know better than to end
What only I could start!

BECAUSE I'M THE ONE AND ONLY
THE MENACING, ROAMING, PSYCHO, GREAT ODE!

Why do I even bother? Bother, BOTHER, Bother, bother, bother?

Why do I even try?
WHY?
Is it just to fill my life
with something, ANYTHING before I die?

Why do I try to love you?
Why do I do all these loving things
hoping to reach the very core of you?
Is it somehow to atone for _my_ confounding sins?

Sins I commit again and again
In my manic desperation to have a friend.
A friend trustworthy enough to be my lover
who'll love in the open and please me undercover.

Why do I even bother
to give you love and respect?
While you treat me like all the others,
crude and low down; utterly reckless.

It must be plain to you
that I have no sense.
What else does a man do
once a woman reveals the suspense?

Once the suspense of need and want
are staged for the world to see;
no need for you to bother
to voice, to act, to play the romantic lead.

No, you don't even care
to be the director, producer, or some lowly stagehand.
Your predatory manly fears
keep you from being a complete, whole man.

So why do I bother
to try to entice, appease, please you?
Why do I even bother
to think that you could grow, learn and live...
because of the things I do?

AFRAID

Afraid.
Afraid to push.
Afraid to say.
Afraid to not say anything.
Afraid to get in my own way.

Afraid to upset you,
Afraid you'll pull away.
Afraid I've already fallen for you;
Afraid you don't feel the same way.
Afraid deeply to be afraid.
Fear only makes us weak.
But afraid, I am, to come on too strong.
Afraid to max out at some low peak.

Afraid to give all my thoughts and energy to you
Afraid even if I give my love, my time,
My emotions, my all – it just won't do.
Did you come equipped to join me on this climb?
Afraid though, to pull away.
Afraid to turn it off or even slow it down.
So do you think it's' all one big play?
Am I just another gem in your crown?

You have me afraid to love you
Because I know you're afraid to love me.
Before you, "AFRAID" was never a 'thing' I could do.
Now "AFRAID" leads me effortlessly.

So afraid to call,
Afraid to kiss, hug, make love at all.
Afraid to hope, afraid to care.
Afraid I'm wide open but you won't share.
Afraid to want you too much.
Afraid I quiver too easily from your touch.
Afraid you've already lost interest.

Afraid any time now, you'll yell "DISMISSED!"

Afraid, maybe, you still love her.
Afraid, I'm just a big experiment.
Afraid none of my fantasies shall ever occur.
Afraid all my motions won't even make a dent.
Yet afraid to give up,
As my emotional investment is large already.
Afraid, "any which way", I'll mess up!
Afraid, in end, you won't be my reality!

Afraid to stop, afraid to move.
Afraid if I do you'll get with the groove.
Afraid deep down you do love me,
But also afraid, you're just testing me.

Now I'm afraid to pass
And more afraid to fail.
Afraid if successful - it won't last.
Afraid if I fail, you'll run away – FAST!!!.

I'm Not!

I'm not going to show you the way to love.
I'm not going to be patient.
I'm not going to throw myself into it
While you wait around to see what the gods have sent.

I'm not going to give you assurances galore.
I'm not going to be home every time you call.
I'm not going to shut my mouth
When you haven't given it your all.

I'm not going to cry anymore.
I'm not going to overreact to your inaction.
I'm not going to beg to come over
To spend time with you if you have reservations.

But, I'm not going to give up on your ability to love.
Still I'm not going to force you to want me.
In fact, I'm not going to think that you
Don't know how to give me love;
You see, that, Foolish, comes naturally.

What does being in love feel like?

What does being in love feel like?
like eating a banana split,
like indulging in it,
with body and soul
like digesting it through every crevice
and every other pore.

I love you
everything about you.
It's come over me,
sometimes easy,
sometimes forcefully,
sometimes stingy-ly
but always over me.

Being in love isn't good for me,
I gain weight, cause I'm content and happy.
I act stupid, overcome with fits of jealousy
No, baby, being in love ain't good for me.

Selfish Desire

Selfish desires don't fight for sensibility.
Selfish desires, instead feast upon waning morality.
Selfish desires lurk and hide, wrestling to come out and see
Your selfish desires that you've been embedding in me.

I'm too wound up to avoid going out of my way to see you.
I'm too hot, to cool my jets as I wait in this stairwell for you.
I'm too naughty, to relent, to succumb back to innocence
instead of seizing you.
I'm too selfish, not to fill my body, with frenzied sensations
from you.

Selfish desires side swipe society's morays.
Selfish desires don't give a dam about "tomorrow is another
day!"
Selfish desires vaults over work, rushing by to play.
Selfish desires confess marital status is just contested fray.

I'm too wound up to...

GOODBYE, GOOD RIDDANCE

It's over now.
Goodbye and good riddance.

I'll play the last dance game with you.
I'll pretend to be your baby.
But in fact, it's too far gone
for me to be your lady.

You had it good.
You had every opportunity.
But you acted like I wasn't good enough;
Like I was something gross and ugly.

Goodbye,
Good riddance.
Goodbye,
Observe your incompetence.
Goodbye,
Check! Was it impotence?
Goodbye,
My time and efforts evolved into nonsense.
Goodbye
Your lines no longer have credence.

GOODBYE, GOOD RIDDANCE

I Longgggg FOR YOU

I long for you,
I crave you so bad.
But I can't call you.
I can't beg, I can't cry, I can't be sad.

And even though I'm in love with you,
I can't call and tell you,
'cause you've made it clear by your actions
that I've failed to give you satisfaction.

Every tissue in my arm
Is pleading to pick up the phone.
But even someone like me has pride –
What if you just want me to leave you alone?

Or worse yet, maybe you enjoy
seeing me make a fool of myself.
How could we then continue on
once I knew I didn't have your respect?

I never dreamt that loving so good
could make a living BEING so unhappy.
With all my wanderings and experiences,
how did I let these emotions defeat me?

I can't stop, I try so hard.
 I WANT to stop thinking of you.
If you call, I'd be outdone;
When you don't, I'm lost without a clue.

So you see it's all in your hands.
I've denigrated into a worthless pile,
a lump of melted clay,
longing for your touch, hungry for your smile.

Self-respect, dignity, pride.

WHAT'S THAT???
I imagine; I pretend to have them,
but one whisper from you and I'd fall flat.

Please, please take me back.
Maybe I am IMPERFECT.
Maybe I'm not quite what you had in mind.
But how could I be your one and only REJECT?

I'll please you!
I'll be your slave, your word I'll obey.
I'll give up my stubbornness.
I'll bend, I'll behave, I'll do whatever you say.

So you see the truth is
there is no pride inside of me.
The only virtue I have left
is knowing that this is one poem that you will never see.

How did LOVE Forsake?

Even though, your kiss made me dizzy and often giddy,
Even as my touch you said, 'made you weak in the knees',
Our love was supposed to be cement block strong
and this relationship was to be
that tanker ship we could safely venture out into the world
on.

No trained troops or mercenary were to come in and invade
our chosen territory.
No corrupt spy was to creep in and leak mementos or
artifacts of our developing story.
No kind of FORCE...NONE...was to be able to penetrate our
barracks.
Who left the gate open for some corrupt version of a Trojan
Horse to attack?

Oh no... oh, please, no
It can't be, say, it isn't so!

HOW? What ills and poisons spewed forth from YOUR
concealed venom?
If anyone was there to protect me from harm, it was to be
you, my astounding phenom.
Instead, the world now mocks my once lovely face and rushes
in to build its case,
as the swirling winds writhe in pain; chanting "How, on
earth, did LOVE Forsake?"

Don't Make No Waves

I'm just like the calm sea
in which no waves are seen.
It's all because I'm so easy.

I'm very much in contrast to the lion's roar.
More like the soft whistle of breeze through the leaves,
together, me and the wind soar.

I'm also often like the rabbit,
never to make unnecessary sounds.
This I was trained through habit.

I'm usually left to wonder
why... unlike the others, I don't lose
hope and courage in time of despair
or shout and curse in time of anger.

Sometimes, I get feelings of anger
but I just keep them contained
and like the other trapped emotions, it just lingers.

I guess I'm strong enough to ruffle the leaves
but as far I can see
my force can't make any waves,
'cause I'm too easy.

Stop it, already...Don't Love-Verb Me.

Don't love verb me,
Cause you don't know what that means.
For love is action and you've drowned in inactivity.

Don't presume to love noun me,
You're notorious for being blasted confounded!
Love is more than some event, object, idea.
It's more that mere fantasy.

You'll attempt to love adjective, you see...
because you think that covers your prime directive.
But your loving way is modified and not good enough for me.

Halt that love adverb sequence you unloaded so cleverly.
Careful! You'll wreck your own nerves trying
to lovingly adverb all things and people in your reach.

"But I Love You"

Stop It! What did I just say, don't you dare
    Don't you dare
    Don't you dare
    love-verb me!

P-E-R-I-O-D!

Calypso's Special Twilight

Foresight
>   Seeing beyond now, beyond me
>   Scanning the future, faux world
>   Way into forthcoming centuries
>   Dancing to their changing melodies
>   Foresight

Hindsight
>   Seeing back then, before me
>   Scanning the ancient, sparring world
>   Way back into past centuries
>   Dancing to their Hephaestus forged melodies
>   Hindsight

Non-sight
>   Not seeing what's coming, happening to me!
>   Not being able to scan the goings-on in my fringed
>   world.
>   Way deep into my flowing streams I seek
>   But can't find my life's dance, my own broken
>   melody.
>   Non-sight

Twilight
>   Seeing all else, everywhere else when I look out
>   beyond me
>   Scanning cuisine, woe, gaiety, assorted cultures in the
>   world
>   Way across their continents, creeks and valleys
>   I can dance telepathically, somehow, to everyone
>   else's melodies.

>   Twilight

The Fake Reveal {Really Surreal}
(...And I stepped into his surreal)

When the surreal becomes real
When real isn't such a good deal

When the deal is deemed only a hidden steal

When the world conspires to make
the hidden steal...the big reveal!

When the big reveal
is just ink on the page that never dried
and his eyes cry for the horizon where his heart lies

This fantastic leisurely voyage was to you surreal
but for me, it's my real.

And the professed love – the show's ... fake reveal.

"And the surprise is...!"
The surprise is surprising just to me. Yep, mine all mine.
The reveal – simply a drape covering up some well-scattered
time.

I slammed, crashed hard, forever scarred, by my re-arranged
real,
but for you, it's just another horse drawn chariot ride,

flying a bit off course because of a bended wheel.
a small dent, a minor detour on an unguided tour,

into the surreal.

EROS, child of Chaos.

Eros, spawn of Chaos.
How naively they confuse
you for a cherub.

Chapter FOUR

Wedged Between the Gods, Destiny and Dreams of Penelope

Love Adjudicated...A woman questions Love

Nestor speaking to Telemachus "If Athene were to take as great a liking to you as she did to Odysseus when we were fighting before Troy (for I never yet saw the gods so openly fond of anyone as Athene then was of your father), if she would take as good care of you as she did of him, these wooers would soon some of them forget their wooing."

The Odyssey, Book III

Wedged Between the Gods, Destiny and Dreams of Penelope

What thus happens to me?
Penelope weaves every day and reliefs every night.
The Morai – the Greek Goddesses of Destiny
plot long and hard over the <u>Great</u> Odysseus' life.
I love you so unconditionally that it dismantles my
reasoning, my seasons, my eternal flight.
Where do I go to be safe,
when wedged between the jealous gods, your pre-spun
destiny and your suddenly renewed dreams of your queen,
Penelope?

AI Image by Canva

Holding this ancient diary
I see and feel...

~ *Quote from The Odyssey, Book I*
"But one man alone...
his heart set on his wife and his return – Calypso,
the bewitching nymph, the lustrous goddess, held him back,
deep in her arching caverns, craving him for a husband."

~ *Quote from The Odyssey, Book IV*
(Old sea-god Proteus tells Menelaus)
"I saw him once on an island, weeping live warm tears
in the nymph Calypso's house – she holds him there by force.
He has no way to voyage home to his own native land,
no trim ships in reach, no crew to ply the oars
and send him scudding over the sea's broad back."

~ *Quote from The Odyssey, Book V*
(Calypso tells Hermes the gods are unfair).
"Hard-hearted you are, you gods!
You unrivaled lords of jealousy –
scandalized when goddesses sleep with mortals,
openly, even when one has made the man her husband."

~ *Quote from The Odyssey, Book V*
(Calypso agrees to Zeus' command).
"But since there is no way for another god to thwart the will
of storming Zeus and make it come to nothing, let the man go
– if the Almighty insists, commands – and destroy himself on
the barren salt sea! I'll send him off, but not with any
escort."

~ *Quote from the Odyssey, Book V*

(Calypso and Odysseus after Hermes visit).
"On the headland, sitting, still, weeping, his eyes never dry,
his sweet life flowing away with the tears he wept for his
foiled journey home, since the nymph no longer pleased. In
the nights, true, he'd sleep with her in the arching cave – he
had no choice – unwilling lover alongside lover all too
willing".

~ *Quote from the Odyssey, Book V*

(Calypso tells Odysseus of her willingness)
"No need, my unlucky one, to grieve here any longer,
no, don't waste your life away. Now I am willing,
heart and soul, to send you off at last."

~ *Quote from the Odyssey, Book V*

(Calypso offers immortality)
"So then, royal son of Laertes, Odysseus, man of exploits,
still eager to leave at once and hurry back to your own home,
your beloved native land?
Good luck to you, even so. Farewell!
But if you only knew, down deep, what pains are fated to fill
your cup before you reach that shore, you'd stay right here,
preside in our house with me and be immortal."

Gods in the Trojan War	
Greece	**Troy**
Athena *(Goddess of Wisdom and Strategic Warfare)*	Ares *(God of War)*
Poseidon *(God of the Seas)*	Artemis *(Goddess of the Hunt)*
Hera *(Queen Goddess, Wife of Zeus)*	Aphrodite *(Goddess of Love)*
Hephaestus *(God of Metal Works, Son of Hera and Zeus)*	Eos *(Goddess Dawn)* *(Mother of Memmon (Warrior from Ethiopia)*
Neutral (?)	
Zeus *(King of the Olympian Gods)* Hermes *(Messenger God)* Nemesis *(Goddess of Rightful Retribution)*	

Major Heros in the Trojan War	
Greece	**Troy**
Agamemnon/Menelaus/ Ajax the Great/ Achilles/Patroclus/ Diomedes/Odysseus	Hector/Paris/Aeneas/ Memnon/Penthesilea/ Hippolyta

Odysseus' major PERILS during The Odyssey, after the Trojan War
Odysseus' HUBRIS (Excessive Pride and Arrogance) irks the Gods, so he experiences many perils on his sea route home to Ithaca.
End of Trojan War: Odysseus' lack of proper recognition and burnt offerings to the Greek gods who helped him.
Cyclops Polyphemus: Odysseus and his men are trapped in the cave of this one-eyed giant. They blind him and sneak out, hiding behind his enormous sheep. Polyphemus, who was Poseidon's son, complained that Odysseus had wounded him and then taunted him.
Sirens: Female singing entities that lured men with enchanting music and voices. Odysseus had his ears plugged with beeswax to resist their call.
Scylla and Charybdis: Scylla, a six-headed monster and Charybdis, a massive whirlpool.
Circe: Goddess and her nymphs who turned Odysseus' men into pigs with magic.
Underworld (Hades): Odysseus goes to Hades to get information from a prophet named Tiresias and sees his mother while there.
The Cattle of Helios: Odysseus' men slaughtered the sacred cattle of the sun god Helios. To punish them Zeus destroys the ship and only Odysseus survives.
Calypso: "Right?" They say held captive by me on my island Ogygia but was ordered to be let go by Zeus. Yea, yea – the message was delivered by Hermes.

Criticize

The people of today,
those of whom I see,
who think themselves gods,
sit around.
Someone comes along
who refuses to sit down.
She becomes active.
She doesn't just
sit, chat and criticize,
but rather extends her creativity
by doing.
Thus, those who sat down
in the beginning
Still sit,
and now they have
a new 'he-said', 'she-said' topic of discussion.

UNINSPIRED SEED

Proteus, jealous old man of the sea, splashing by –
awashed in whirlpools of insatiable curiosity,
Your sticky wagging tongue is known for creating
odysseys of kings reclaiming vast legacies.

Prometheus, brave but
silly titan 'jone-ing' on Zeus.
Goofing up – granting man fire;
to dine on more than nuts and fruit.
Pandora, young girl, prancing by,
erupting from their male engorged visions,
so naïve and with no mentor
found corrupting hope - life's hidden treasure.
Poor me, lonely Calypso, lost in your vacuous eyes,
Begging your pardon, and for early release.
Why swallow me whole, sequester my pride?
Will your trumped-up charges never cease?

Proteus and other acclaimed tongue-waggers,
Will you continue on, still for centuries more,
re-hashing such scenes for your tedious amusement?
Sucking life-force from neophytes across the
eons of life...always NEVER full, amiably malcontent?

Aphrodite, Every Man's Dream

Aphrodite, every man's dream carried by the seasons
in our collective consciousness. Love's pure embodiment
-spirit, beauty and sexual generation. Venus!

She, who sprang, forth
out of the foam, swarming the sea.
A full manifestation of memory and destiny,
sky-god Uranus' genital piercing the heavens
splashing forcefully on man's terrain
as his youngest, titan son, Cronus got even.

Aphrodite, the most beautiful amongst the beautiful
burst through those lusty droppings,
re-mixing the gods' most dire fall.
Foam, frothy and rich, sensuously thick
bonded with the oceans' mutable molecules,
until her tender firmness was fixed,
until her brain ran massive and quick
until Aphrodite's femininity dripped heavy, moist and slick.

Aphrodite, every man's dream carried by the seasons
in our collective consciousness. Love's pure embodiment
-spirit, beauty and sexual generation. Venus!

Discordia and the Apple of Discord
(a speech)

*I am the Goddess Discordia, so called by the 'ancient'
Romans in their juvenile, imitation mythology.*

*But if you check the more authentic Greek Mythology, I am
the irresistible, irreplaceable, iridescent Goddess Eris.
ERIS – GODDESS OF CHAOS, Goddess of DISCORD,
Goddess of STRIFE.*

*Personally I find such labeling to be so belittling and so
confining. I mean which Greek God or Goddess didn't
create some chaos. After all, you have ARES - God of War, if
that's not discord -- what IS? You have naughty Aphrodite
and her baby son shooting those misdirected arrows of love
all over the place, causing trouble.*

*Look at Zeus, King of the Gods, how many times did he come
to earth from Mount Olympia to score with some nymph only
to cause generations of discord and strife?*

*Speaking of nymphs, it's because of a sea nymph named
Thetis that you remember me at all.*

*See, Zeus was doing his usual sneaking around on Queen
Goddess Hera when he saw and fell for Thetis, a sea-nymph.
HA HA she wasn't even a real sea nymph but a river nymph.
PHATETIC!!*

*To cover it all up, Zeus got King Peleus of Thessaly to marry
her.
Now he was FINE!*

Here's where I come in.

*All the invitations are sent out but Zeus bans ME from the
wedding! He says I'm a mischief maker and I cause discord*

and disharmony everywhere I go.
Can you believe he snubbed me? *This is the wedding of the ages, I mean gods, goddesses, kings, rich single eligible mortals everywhere; everybody who's anybody was going to be there!*

THIS IS PROBABLY THE FIRST RECORDED SNUB IN HISTORY!

Well, I'm still a good sport so I think I'll just do something creative, maybe a little arts & craft.

I crafted this beautiful golden apple and inscribed it "THE PRETTIEST" and oops it just tumbles away from me and rolls down the hallway into the dance hall room of this uppidity wedding.

Guess what? Let me tell you right now, it's vanity, ego, and jealousy that create discord, Not Me!

See the 3 Power Goddesses, well you know; in some would-be era there'll be Super Models (isn't that right)? {same kind of vibe}.

So Hera, Queen of the gods, Athena - Goddess of wisdom, and Aphrodite - Goddess of love all fight, I mean fist fight over the apple!

Weak "Father Zeus" is a "scare-dy" cat. He's afraid to judge the contest and picks a little shepard boy, a mortal from the land of Troy named Paris to be the arbitrator.

Poor Paris, he gets involves and his little world will never be the same.

My apple, heretofore known as the "Apple of Discord", or more affectionately "the Golden Apple" starts "THE CATFIGHT" of all time.

I mean Hera offers Paris wealth and power.
Athena offers the boy wisdom,
and Aphrodite offers him the most beautiful woman in the
world.

The lad chose the most beautiful woman in the world, Helen,
but there's a technicality. She's not really available. She's
married to the powerful Greek King Menelaus of Sparta,
whose comrade is the cunning King Odysseus of Ithaca (after
whom the tale the Odyssey is written). Anyway, as you
know, the rest is history.

Paris kidnaps Helen and whisks her away to Troy and then
there's ten years of the Trojan War—which left you such fond
legacies as the Trojan Horse and Achilles' heel...strange
Achilles was the offspring of the wedding that started all this.

But more importantly and the point I've spent eternity trying
to make is that just about all the Gods participated in the
Trojan War in some form or the other, all to their own
amusement.

So NOW do you see, how they tried to pin all of this on poor
little me?

TODAY,
I'm finally ready to go on record after these many thousand
of years and tell YOU the TRUTH.

I simply meant my beautiful golden apple as a wedding gift
for the lovely bride. It's that simple.

That's my story and I'm sticking to it.

I am your goddess ERIS – Discordia and this is
the "Apple of Discord".

IN DEATH
(Odysseus recalls seeing his mother in Hades)

Stood There

        Let him

               come as he willed

In fact,

        Forced him

             to enter.

Now

        that memory recalls.

What

        an easy way out....

Out of a place

        where being lonely

             raced me to death.

Yet in death

        loneliness brings my soul...

             ...happiness.

GIVES ME PEACE OF MIND.

Ulysses, Nestled in My Lap

Drift off to fluid, floating, freeing oceans.
Ahoy!
Approach anxiously, nay gingerly. Land at night, most
covertly
Upon that majestic, tailored land you summon your own.
Dream of young maidens strangling breadth in fresh lace
corsets,
Of crusty old men, mangy dogs in tow,
Hurrying to catch the rhythmic verses of your aching lament,
   -   **Do so, your always-regal head, nestled in my lap.**

Yea tell all who will listen,
That I bound you; had you shackled to me,
An earth-bound goddess, stowed away on an island of
fantasy,
Far beyond the glare and midst of Mount Olympus,
Held your brutal, "warringness", silent and powerless,
Seething your manly body heat, depth and breadth
Harnessed to my chest,
Gauging the rise and fall of my heaving breasts
For seven inexplicable years, nay an eternity
Right from whence you stumbled free
On my near Africa beach, upon my eager shore,
Fresh from your 'pride before the fall'...
Ah, too late...and 'winners take all', Trojan brawl.
   -   **Recall it all; your crafty cunning head nestled in my
       lap.**

Paint a tortured picture of your entrapment,
Sing a long Homeric song of your broken heart epic.
Blame me for your lustful, sultry gaze bruising the epidermis
Of my olive soaken skin,
Of your power tool crated appendages exceeding
performance
Standards every summer like night
In the inner vestiges of my Aphroditeque designed castle-inn.

Claim diligently that I was at fault
So that you dare not break away,
How I used my potent godly,
Worse yet, interwoven divine womanly powers,
Awashed in forbidden skills
To keep you
Treacherous, crafty, inventor of the Trojan horse – you
On the terra cotta, limestone floors of my island den.
Conceive it all now, your princely Machiavelli, nay,

- *Cunning Ulysses' head, nestled in my lap.*

FORWARD MARCH!
(Athena speaks!)

DON'T GET BOGGED DOWN
IN THE TRIVIA OF THEIR LIVES.
DON'T STOP THINKING FOR YOURSELF,
IT JUST ISN'T WISE!

STAND UP FOR EVERYTHING DEAR TO YOU.
NOT JUST THE OBVIOUS, THE NEEDED, THE FEW.
*BUT FOR YOURSELF, **YOUR HISTORY**, **YOUR***
***FUTURE**.*
DON'T END UP JUST ANOTHER HAPLESS CREATURE.

IT'S EASY TO BE SWEET TALKED INTO MEDIOCRITY.
IT'S HARD AS HELL TO STAY THE COURSE,
PARTICULARLY SINCE VALUES CHANGE WITH
SEASONALITY.
*YOU HAVE TO USE YOUR POWER; **YOU ARE THE***
***FORCE**!*

DON'T BE CONTENT WITH THEIR DREAMS.
***YOU CAN DO MORE** THAN THEIR MINDS HAVE EVER*
SEEN.
LET GO
OF THESE MIDDLE OF THE ROAD COMFORTS.
RE-EMBARK ON YOUR JOURNEY; ABANDON THIS
DESERT!

FORWARD MARCH....!

RAMBLING
(The Iliad / The Trojan War)

*...I'm rambling on...trying to decipher ...why? Why has this
ball of wax landed in <u>my</u> life?
Like fleet footed Hermes, appeared to Paris, a mere shepherd
boy on Mount Ida, telling him to choose amongst the three
heralded goddesses, to declare the most beautiful....*

*Like Paris, dazzled by Aphrodite's radiance, whose golden
girdle forced him to grant her the cherished apple over
Queen Hera and Athena the wise,*

*Like Paris – put out by his mother Hecuba,
reared by the slave Agelaus,
but suckled by a bear,*
> *Only to return to Troy,
> ultimately to seize Helen
> to fulfill the prophesy of a flaming torch
> which set afire the entire city of Troy,
> burning to ash.*
*If only they had yielded to the gift
 of his sister's Cassandra's prophecy,
instead of reuniting the family.*

*Athena and Hera, angrily turned their backs and swore
vengeance upon Paris, his father King Piram and Troy and
all its people.*

*At first, they say, Paris could not say who was the most
beautiful. Yes, Athena and Hera indubitably vied for the title
in the contest of young Paris giving Eris' golden apple,
inscribed "To The Most Beautiful".*

*No. Loveliest of Lovelies, Aphrodite was victor but Athena,
 it seems, has the last laugh!
While Aphrodite rules over love
Athena simply rips ours apart,*

casting a dagger from heaven into my jaded heart.

Menelaus, king of Sparta by marrying Helen,
Menelaus, whose brother was Agamemnon, King of Mycenae
whose wife Clytemnestra is Helen's stepsister, (another
cursed inlet into this tale)

Was it not you, crafty Odysseus who had all, swear to
Helen's stepfather Tyndareus, then King of Sparta (but who
probably didn't need that protection for all know that her
real father is the almighty Zeus),

Was it not you, Odysseus providing your wise counsel,
demanded from all the suitors, of this the most beautiful
woman, known to man,
an oath that with his weapon he would defend her chosen
bridegroom against anyone who posed any hostility,
once she married?

Strange, how Paris who voyaged there to Greece to assuage
his father, King Priam's grief for the prior generation's
abduction of Priam's sister, Hesione that led to your
wayward journey.
So Paris, like any newly reunited child,
hoping to bring his father joy,
led a great fleece to Greece, journeying there to rescue
Hesione
from King Telamon of Salamis,
even though he had married her
and made her his lawful wife and queen. Still, there
languished the pain
of a loved one being carried off, for they say
Hercules who killed Laomedon,
carried off Hesione and gave her to Telamon.

Consequently, while Menelaus was away in Pylos,
The prince landed on Cythera to make an offering at the
Temple of Artemis.

Paris, dressed in sumptuous robes of purple and gold,
was mesmerized by Helen, as she entered the sanctuary
whose beauty is said-told to rival Aphrodite's.

Paris then entered Sparta. Queen Helen, received him with
the hospitality due to strangers
and the royal treatment due to the son of Kings.
Paris, masterfully skilled on the lyre,
reflected such sweetness, grace and love,
overwhelming the unguarded heart of Helen.

So seeing her there, he could only remember Aphrodite's
promise
of marrying the most beautiful woman in the world...that
could only be Helen! Helen! Helen!

Hence, forgetting his original purpose he later stormed the
palace,
took all of Menelaus' worldly riches that he could carry and
carried off
what appeared to be, a resisting Helen. Rumor has it,
she actually followed him to his fleet, not so much against
her will
and once on some island called Cranae, she consented to be
his, all his.

Light-hearted Helen, so light she abandoned her baby girl,
Hermione
to sail off for this whirlwind romance with Paris.
Self-indulgent Helen, who was used to being rescued,
Oh yes, remember how Theseus had abducted her as a child,
and her brothers Castor and Polydeuces had brought her
home again.

Thus, all of Helen's former suitors, along with all other
nobles of Greece,
raced to Menelaus' cry for vengeance,
hence launching a thousand ships.

In fact, even her brothers Castor and Polydeuces,
(I preferred to call him Pollux myself)
those glorious sons of Leda by 'swan' disguised Zeus
once again
headed out but their ship sank at Lesbos and their father,
Zeus
placed them in the sky, forming that constellation of stars,
Gemini, to protect all sailors and their ships.
(Oops, did they let you slip?)

Only Odysseus and Achilles held back
from joining the campaign.
Yes, you crafty Odysseus didn't want
to leave your wife, Penelope and newborn son, Telemachus.

You acted like you had gone crazy, even yoked an ox
and an ass and plowed your field (that's a funny one),
using salt instead of seed in the furrows.
Ha, Ha! But Palamedes, who had been sent to fetch you,
devised a scam of his own,
placing your beloved Telemachus in the field to be plowed.
Sure thing, you lifted the plow just there. It was clear your
' shenanigans' were just a ploy and
you "wiliest of all mortals" were forced
to keep the oath - you, yourself had first invoked!

Then, there was heartthrob, Achilles, the most splendid!
Son of Peleus and Thetis – another launching pad for this
war and subsequent odyssey
(see Discordia and the Apple of Discord)
Thetis, by quivering him in celestial fire or dipping in the
River Styx
hoped to make her child immortal armouring him except for
his heel.
Trying to avert a tragedy of a prophesy, she had
Achilles specially reared. Deemed delicate, was disguised
and brought upas a girl
by King Lycomedes on the island of Scyros.

But when what appeared to be enemies approached,
he did not flee, like the other girls, but grabbed his shield
and spear and hence was off with educator Phoenix
and dear friend Patroclus to fight at the Trojan War,
all to reclaim faithless Helen and all the male egos involved.

But there's so much more to this mythological lore.

Other mighty warriors took their place, like guess who?
Yes, mighty Ajax, son of...? Yes, son of Telamon and
Hesione. Whew wee, ooo!
It's tougher than melting wax,
it's like megalith stone forced for glue.

Of course, Agamemnon was chosen commander in chief.

So like Achilles pleaded for Iphigenia's life,

I'm rambling on...trying to decipher ...why has this ball of
wax landed in my life?

But everyone knows, well, everyone knows now
that leadership requires personal sacrifice.
So boastful Agamemnon, shot Artemis' sacred hind
and offended her by saying even she,
Artemis, goddess of the hunt, could do no better.
Thus, Artemis demanded he sacrifice his daughter,
Iphigenia, or else the Argives
(Greeks) would not get the winds needed
to sail their warring fleet from Aulis to Troy.

So Agamemnon summoned his fair daughter supposedly
to be betrothed to Achilles, yet Achilles was already married.
Mommy dearest, Clytemnestra came along with baby son,
Orestes in tow...
...so this leads to another Greek tragedy – " how I crave a
comedy"...
...Agamemnon returned home with victory over Troy,

to Clytemnestra who detested him for killing her girl-child,
to be killed himself by Clytemnestra and her lover, Aegisthus
who were then later to be destroyed by Orestes,
who then was hunted by vengeful Furies -, but yes

Like Achilles pleading for Iphigenia's life...

Like Artemis secretly switching a hind
on the altar on which brave and dedicated Iphigenia
volunteered to lie.

...So have my deeds, words and name been forevermore
sacrificed.

**I'm rambling on and on...trying to decipher ...why has this
ball of wax landed in my life?**

But you Odysseus, you too, did your dirty deeds.
No, need to run and hide,
My uncles were Foresight (Prometheus) and
Hindsight (Epimetheus)
and besides, all the gods gossip. You know that's right!

Was it not you Odysseus who abandoned
Philoctetes on the island of Lemnos,
deep in its cave rather than smell his rotting flesh?
As the Argives journeyed on to war, to Troy?

And was it not til nine years later in the grip of defeat,
following the death of Achilles,
that you were forced to retreat since the seer told the Greeks
that they could not win, without the unerring arrows
bequeathed him by Hercules?
Didn't you have Achilles's son, Neoptolemus venture back
there to deceive him,
but for Neoptolemus speaking the truth, Philoctetes' old
friend, Hercules appeared from the heavens to assure him it
was all the will of the gods?

Back in Troy, the once isolated and stranded, now fully
restored Philoctetes shot his spear
wounding Paris in his groin, sending him back to Mount Ida
and the wife, Oenone,
he'd abandoned; had left behind "to take pleasure in Helen's
eternal youth".
Tell me, isn't all this part of your famous quote
"Experience has taught me
that words often succeed more readily than deeds" sense of
the truth?

And Odysseus, was it not you in your meanness and anger
that betrayed Palamedes?
Palamedes, who outsmarted you when you wanted to renege
on your oath,
the oath that you devised that sent so many men away from
their lives,
their wives and their families?
For all those years, you still resented and vowed to fatally
wound him, your personal enemy.
Alas, when honored Palamedes was chosen by Apollo to
bring the hecatomb
the sun-god demanded once the great Argive counsel refused
to release the daughter of
Chryses back home to her father, priest of Phoebus Apollo,
your envy forced itself up like red hot lava spouting over
white, cold boulders of rock.
This memory of Chryseis' tale, rather clearly illustrates,
wouldn't you say,
so clearly the thread about lovers who willfully detained their
enslaved lovers,
no matter whether in Tartarus, Olympus or Terra, it fumes.
Still, how far away, back in the trenches of war, the truth now
looms.
You drafted a letter, supposedly written by the Trojans,
concealed gold in Palamedes' hut and magically had him
found out as a traitor.
His fate was sealed and he was stoned to death, this is

another in the long line of reasons
you've been cursed on your journey home, because right
there and then Nemesis vowed vengeance.

Detainees and captors...not unlike Briseis who was fetched
from the war-house of Achilles, by Agamemnon,
effectively derailing the war.
Prime example of hostage taking and super fragile egos...
...So blast Homer for spreading rumors ABOUT ME and
millennia of disparaging remarks!

If only I had the magic voice of Orpheus,
Would the male storytellers, Proteus supposedly to Menelaus,
Menelaus to your son Telemachus accompanied by Athena
disguised as Mentor, and of course, Homer,
would they tell what was right about us?

So, yes, Odysseus, the muse in me forces me to accept the
good with the bad
and I recognize that war and its treachery are irreversibly
sad, so
I give you credit for speaking to Achilles to make him rejoin
the war effort,
as Hector, regal son of Priam, brother of Paris
approached the Greek wall and ships.

Like another Greek warrior said in the midst of battle,
"Choose Odysseus, whose heart is steadfast in danger
and who is beloved by Pallas Athena."
Isn't that the truth?
All these years here with me, your heart was steadfastly
joined to your land of Ithaca,
Moreover, all creation knows, even though she proclaims to
be a virgin
That Athena's 'heart bleeds' for you,
She said that herself in pleading your release
from my 'blandishments' to her father Zeus.

'Blandishments", what crime did I commit?
'Blandishments' she says,
well 'blandishments' are just what....Olympian words?
For enticements, for romancing and any woman in love
would entice a man away from leaving her side
And would show love in just about any way.
That does not equate to "detain", to hold captive
To keep against his will, everyone knows with Poseidon
angry,
you could never have sailed away.
But how could she know about experiencing love
Since she's never held a man in her arms that way?
I guess it hard to get there, when your life begins by
springing out of Zeus' head
Instead of through a woman's tunnel of love, deep and well
spread.
But even I know better than to fight with warlike Athena,
Just look at what her jealousy brought upon once precious
Medusa.

Oh yeah...poor Medusa started life as...some say... an
ordinary mortal girl but
her beauty caught Poseidon's attention and he seduced her in
Athena's temple.
Athena, already jealous of her, punished whom? Not the
strong dominant male.
Oh no, she turned her fury on Medusa, turning her into a
Gorgon,
a female monster with a headful of snakes for hair.
Poor thing, joined immortal gorgons Stheno and Euryale,
born of Phorcys and Ceto.
Of course, that wasn't bad enough, Athena continued to
punish Medusa,
aiding Perseus as he hunted her down and chopped off her
head,
which was only good for turning men into stone, anyway.
Perseus used her head over and over again to his own
advantage

*and then turned it over to Athena who placed it into her
shield.
Athena, had flayed off Medusa's skin at her death and turned
it into her trademark, Aegis.*

*Of course, my already condemned father, Atlas got caught up
in the heroic fare.
It wasn't enough that as one of the Titans who lost in the
great war back around the start of time that he had to hold
up the sky.
Ovid's legend decreed that he was king of Mauretania,
an African kingdom lying at the edge of the world,
the land of the Garden of Hesperides, ... you got it...
where Eris' Golden Apple...
probably came from. Well, right after Perseus slew
Medusa's head, Perseus sought shelter there. Citing a
prophecy,
that a son of a Zeus would steal the apples, Atlas refused.
And the fool, pretending to give daddy a gift, took out
Medusa's head, turning mountainous Atlas into stone.
I don't care for their divergent fantasies,
either way his spirit still holds up the skies and
Mount Atlas reigns on!*

*So you see, my soul has the layers to sort out the beauty from
the monstrous ugly.
When Perseus took off Medusa' head, beautiful, winged
horse Pegasus and his mysterious sibling Chrysaor,
her children by Poseidon, did spring forth.*

Anyway, back to the dam war, that brought you here.

*Like Achilles said when speaking to this mother Thetis,
Following his friend Patroclus' death
"Cursed by ANGER, whether it spring in gods or men,
for first it is sweet as honey to the heart, but then it grows
acid as smoke."*

Ladies and Gentlemen, the glory making Trojan War!...
Hector, the pride of Troy and Paris' brother, killed
Patroclus, Achilles friend,
Achilles killed Prince Hector and dragged around his body,
Paris shot Achilles in his vulnerable heel, guided by God
Apollo.
Ajax killed himself for not winning Achilles' armor at the
funeral games.
Odysseus, you did somehow honorably defend Ajax's burial,
normally not granted for one who takes his own life.
But I guess it was the least you could do, seeing they gave the
cherished armor to you.
Of course, Athena was one of the judges...why is that not so
surprising?

Strangely, it was as the losses stacked up that diversity
weaved into this tale.
Queen of the Amazons, Penthesilea (fathered by God Ares)
had arrived to help the Trojans right after Hector was gone.
With twelve chosen companions, and seeking relief from the
Furies
for accidentally killing her beloved sister Hippolyte,
she restored the confidence of the Trojan soldiers who
disseminated by Hector's death could not rally forth.
She enjoyed a spelled of brilliant victory
But once Achilles returned to the field, she answered destiny
and die in a blaze of glory.
Achilles removing her helmet, himself grieved for she was so
noble and lovely.

Next, came Memnon, the Ethiopian,
from the land of black men,
for King Priam had sent for him.
Memnon was the son of the Goddess Eos,
the goddess of dawn.
With his presence the Trojans' hearts grew lighter. Dressed
in his armor,
they say he resembled the grandeur of Ares himself.

The Trojans and Ethiopians fought side by side against the Achaeans.
He fought like a divine conqueror. All changed once he slew the youth,
Antilochus who tried to protect his father, Nestor.
So gentlemanly was he, Memnon respectfully addressed this elder,
as though he was speaking to his own father.
Nestor retreated but Achilles was summoned to engage in hand-to-hand combat.
The gods delighted in this combat from Mount Olympus as the two used swords,
stones and lances and both refused to be diminished by their equally eager stubbornness.
The Fates decided in the end that Achilles thrust his lance into Memnon's breastplate.
He died and his mother covered the earth in darkness. Her other children, the winds
then whisked his body through the air and buried it on the banks of the Aesepus.
Memnon' men in sorrow, thus did retreat and the Trojans and Greeks
Were once again on their own.

Once, these unsung heroes died, then so did Achilles.
Finally, did both men and gods grieve.
Zeus gave the immortals permission to help Troy or Greece.
For the Greeks – Hera, Athena, Poseidon, Hermes, Hephaestus
For the Trojans – Apollo, Artemis, Ares - god of war, Leto, Aphrodite, Eos and Scamander (Xanthus)
And "through both host alike stormed ERIS, the goddess of Discord".

That's when you Odysseus set out to recruit Achilles' son Neoptolemus
and retrieve Philoctetes. After Paris' death, the Greeks stormed Troy.

*Their wall seemed impenetrable and there, you, Odysseus at
the urging of Calchas,
the seer, you devised a ruse, the treacherous Trojan Horse.*

*The bravest of you huddled in the belly of the beast.
The rest docked at Tenedos, burning all the Greek camps
before they left.
You cleverly left Sinon, to act as a dejected cast away. He
persuaded the Trojans,
that the Greeks went home defeated, but to honor Pallas
Athena
they left the great prize, the Trojan Horse; wooden.
Indeed, a priest of Troy tried to warn
his people but two serpents of the ocean sent by Poseidon,
seized him and the Trojans believed it, a good omen to
receive their prize.
All day the Trojans rejoiced, accepting the gift within their
city ramparts.
Under the cover of night, your men descended from its belly,
flung open the gates,
letting in your comrades who had returned to shore and
Troy's doom was sealed.
Oh, if it were not for you Odysseus, where would the Greeks
be,
and how on earth did all this gravitate towards me?*

*Helen, forgiven by Menelaus, was rescued once again!
While all of Troy was burnt down, the men slain with
children and women
forced into slavery and all Troy's riches stolen.
But Ajax of Loris, stormed Athena's temple and captured her
priestess Cassandra,
the sister of Hector and Paris. Once, the Argives set upon the
seas, angry Athena
used Zeus' thunderbolts to destroy, with Poseidon's help,
much of the fleet.
Then, came the justice for your stoning of innocent
Palamedes.*

Even with rains of extreme torrent, his father King Nauplius of Euboea
saw the fleet approaching his coast. He quickly had his people set up torches
along the cliffs on the dangerous side of his island's shores.
Many of the Greeks, summoning to these false beacons of safety crashed and wrecked.
There was scattered many of the dreams and hopes of the Greeks who longed to return home.
And then for special effect....

you Odysseus, the most special case!

Forgive me for bringing this all up...but I'm just rambling on and on...trying to decipher
...why has this ball of wax landed in my life?

Scrambling
(The Odyssey)

What can I say
You tried to make a mad dash out of there
So proud of the Trojan Horse that you conceived via the
insights
of Athena and likely Poseidon, the master of horses.
But how did you fare?

But you were you, boasting all the way home
And you offered some burnt offerings to the Olympians but
You know them, they always want more

*So here you are scrambling because of your **HUBRIS***
The truly one thing that those Olympians can not stand
*– **Human Arrogance.***

Let's see
You and your crew tried to raid the land of the Cicones
but their army drove you back,
Yes mighty warrior-king, that remains a fact.

The Lotus Eaters – created such a desire, your men didn't
want to return home.
But that place could not be your ultimate landing zone.

You blinded the sea god Poseidon's Cyclops son Polyphemus
and had to brag about it on the way out of his cave.
You really didn't expect sore Poseidon to make a fuss?

Then, your reckless crew, open Aeolus' bag of winds
But greed often seems like the most ridiculous sin.

Those cannibalistic Laestrygonia, ate and ate. Didn't you
leave Troy with 600 men and twelve ships?
Story goes you dragged your ass out of there with only one

ship.

*Everyone knows about you and Circe and how she turned
your men into pigs.
Then Hermes rescued you from that magic and you then
spent a year there. Oops, Ithaca wasn't that urgent!?!*

*Of course, you visited Hades to gain prophecies
But ran into Mommy Anticlea who despised time's atrocities.*

*Sailed by the sirens and was so full of mystery and lust
But that's standard for the course, isn't it Odysseus?*

*In that narrow strait of survival between Scylla and
Charybdis
You sacrificed more of your men,
so you yourself could avoid the abyss.*

*Your men slaughtered and ate the sacred cattle
of the ancient sun god Helios.
That thunderbolt from Zeus wrecked the remaining ship and
let you know that Zeus was dead serious.*

*So everything gained and everyone allied is now gone
Only you Odysseus, only you, got to move on.*

*Onto Ogygia, and lovely, lonely Calypso
But in the end, you said you were detained,
So where can loving reminiscences take path and flow?*

*Who knows? Onto Ino and Nausicaa you'll go.
The rich Phaeacians fill you with treasures and gold to*

finally steal away home.

Home to loving Penelope, being courted by a raging gang.
But you fought and won, and reign again,
the Mighty Odysseus
In your own land!

DEHORS!

DEHORS, MAINTENANT!
JE PREFER QUE TU PARTS! SURE!
TU VA CHEZ TA FEMME.

BIG BANGED

*Theory. The theory of the expanding universe has become
our befuddled story.*

*Together, we emerged, we ruled, we consumed all energy, all
mass.*

*We formed the cosmos, the universe in its orderly,
harmonious whole.*

*Internal combustion? Violent Gases? Spewed us forth into
separate fractions.*

*As time, that contemptible element passed by, both you and I,
lost our senses.*

*Now the universe spins around. What was once solid, silent is
now speed, sound.*

*What was once one – is - now many forms evolved; entities
like light and gravity.*

*Each moment, is an eternity of longed-for memories, of the
joyous time when we were "unison"*

*and cared nothing for resistance. How strong and weak we
grow now, our own powerful solar systems,*

on alternate edges of the ever-expanding universe.

*With each sub-minuet of a nanosecond, you speed light-years
away from me.*

You're so far away from me, the naked eye can't see.

*The Big Bang Theory – is that how the universe was born?
Is that the so-called beginning of dawn?*

It's the epoch of you and me as we spread out; increase.

*How does growth, evolving, developing – equate – to being
free? Not being free?*

Big Banged.

CATASTROPHE

Could there be...are there any survivors?
Must target the roving bands of liars, thieves, loiterers.
What phenomenon garnered such abject devastation?
What ungodly creature dismembered God's own creation?

Ravenous rivers raging, onerous oceans oscillating,
malicious mountains moving, dangerous dams deteriorating.
Stalwart walls crumbling, bruised lips swollen,
tired eyes blackened, ardent spirits broken.

Who can survive this? If only
I had another wish....even if the damage weren't enough,
There's disease now, there's hunger –
everything is blessed with a curse!

Catastrophe - hurricane, typhoon, hardened lava,
tornado, gale force winds, tsunami, flooded areas,
Nauseous pillars, clouds of smoke,
frozen terrain; dying memories, crippled hope.

Heartwarming homes once stock full of love
stuck beneath acres of grudging mud.
Cherished temples honoring gifts from above,
floating; splintered in the muck of the flood.

Collapsing lungs, choked off by reeking fumes.
Battered arms, hustling to earth/unearth tombs.
Rescue squads lost, wandering aimlessly without a clue.
Hangers-on; praying, grieving, expecting whom?

One day Troy, the Philippines, Louisiana, Mt. Vesuvius,
one day, Montserrat, Haiti, Florida, Honduras.
Entrapment, middle passage, slavery,
confinement, loss lineage....*HUMANITY!*

How do I start over?
Is there enough fresh water to cleanse my wounds?
Where do I start, to put it all back together?
Who is this eternal name, throughout the ages, called Noah?

Catastrophe. What a coy, sensuous term
to express how our lives have been overturned.
What discipline, what inlay of strategy/ systems
will rescue me from the land of the condemned?

So like the life spent loving him,
So like the hurricane thrashed the light within.
So like the flood wrestled with the wind,
So like the tornado triumphs in sin.
So like the avalanche crushed my heart,
So like the volcano burned away every spark.
So like the typhoon ripped my vessel apart,
So like he scurried away so my demise could start.

Catastrophe.
So much loss, untold misery, forever agony…
*All because - I chose… **to love somebody**.*
How did the world turn on me?

Unraveling & Traveling
(The Unbinding of Me)

Someone's daughter, Someone's provider,
Someone's rescuer, Someone's healer

I have to leave this place. I have to holler!

Unraveling through the rings
Traveling through the earthly spins
They place me as one of Saturn's moon,
Ha ha!
Cited a trojan, trailing moon - stuck in a co-orbital loon.

I have to leave this place. I have to holler!

Space isn't big enough
Time isn't fast or slow enough
Thank you Cronos/Saturn for the sojourn
But back to Gaia, to find my closure.

I have to leave this place. I have to holler!

It was fun, sliding, dissipating, and recombining.
Reassembling me into a new mysterious thing.
There's no solid island mass for them to find
Be it off Malta, Gozo, Gavdos or Sicily or the Ionian isles.
Honored to be linked to Egypt and her glorious Nile.

That guy said that Ogygia was in the naval of the sea
So when I splashed down to earth, this time
I remained a mist, a shadow of Ogygia's former floating self
I like it like this. My wholeness is all frequency and chime.

Frequency, vibes and chime, a beautiful immortal soul that's
me.
Frequency, vibes and chime, and even an island music called

Calypso makes me move so free.
Frequency, vibes and chime, a wind instrument circling the
seas.
Frequency, vibes and chime – free from your thoughts
And allowed to be me,
Just me
not just the "Detainer", "the Concealer",
a Temptress, an Archetype
or
a byline in your story

frequency, vibes and chime - unravelling
frequency, vibes and chime - travelling
frequency, vibes and chime - freeing
frequency, vibes and chime - reconstituting

frequency, vibes and chime – a new, renewed goddess
– the legacy of me!
frequency, vibes and chime – a new, renewed goddess
– what a pleasure it has been and it is, to be me!

IMMORTALITY

Immortality
you were offered, but refused.
Proud of you ~ FREE WILL!

Chapter FIVE

Calypso Music

Love Authenticated...A woman vibrates Love

(CALYPSO SAYS TO ODYSSEUS)

"My every impulse bends to what is right. Not iron, trust me, the heart within my breast. I am all compassion."

The Odyssey, Book V

Calypso Music

Divine - earthly queen.
Womanly essence heard;
now and through time, her compassion's seen.
Once setting free the aches
of a diminished, powerful man to the rhythms in her alcove,
anointing his bruises, squalling him relief in concentric
wakes.

Soon buried in legend. Time galloped in, to rescue, restore
her glory.
Her captured spirit, filled of music, again free, floated
across the waves of time.
Helping a people to tell, form, develop their story.
Seeing them ravished by pain and greed and racist pride
Calypso re-emerged from the depths of the sea
to offer spirit, true pride and new release.

For love so profound can't be corked in a bottle forever,
to be unplugged just in heated moments of Homeric debate.
Here, compassion is the true passion, and love is its own
treasure.
Treasure to be celebrated in one man's dreams or ancient
Greece
or to be discovered in the new aquatic streams of the
Caribbean Sea.
Dance, my muses! It's carnival, I'm your Calypso. SET
FREE!

AI Image by Canva

Holding this ancient diary

I sense and experience ...

Calypso's Ogygia

On her island, the wind
pleads entry of her coast,
and pounds his urgentness
on the fragility of her skin,
her skin, whose touch of
divine relief eases
all turbulence, storms,
storms eager to rip apart
unprotected vessels challenging his strength.

What other port bids him release,
a sanctuary to lay his burden down,
unseals her confessional booth
accepting deeds so atrocious,
nature repels? Where else,
soothes his rage, grants him penance
and the will to surge another day?
Praises how he revolutionizes mountain ranges
while gently sprinkling fresh dew, each morning anew?

Showers.   *Shadows.*   *Silhouette.*

Waters cascading over perpetual herb-entwined cliffs.
Sculpted harmony hurting to reunite with cast-away bliss.
These memories cloud my vision.
Your steamy showers mist my renewed life,
Flowing back across the waves to your sexy silhouette.

Fullness. Finding the depth and breadth of lively
amusement.
Treasure chest of island vibes drenched with caresses and
playful excitement.
These memories cloud my vision.
Your steamy showers haze my new, old life.
Digging through the quarry of time to your sexy silhouette.

Luxuriant, pampered arms rubbing my sore limbs down.
Long luscious legs matching my strength pound for pound.
These memories cloud my vision.
Your stormy showers fog my longed for, subdued life.
Circulating, splintered upon my raft, to your sexy silhouette.

Fragrant oils, grape-draped vines, open air nights.
Four running streams of water almost converging, right
into these memories that cloud my vision.
Your steamy showers shadow my fresh, outmoded life;
'Trippin' to dock in your safe harbor,
anchoring onto your sexy shadowy silhouette.

The Love I Was In {Part I}

I was in love a long, long time ago.
He tweaked my keys, he pulled my strings,
But it didn't matter – for it was Love I was in.

I was in love not long ago, not too long ago at all.
My every thought was him,
in my eyes you could see reflections of him
I was blind to everything, but who cared –
it was Love I was in.

I was in love just the other day,
like Friday, half of Saturday, not on Sunday.
He smelled so good, like a slow roasted peanutty wood.
Smelling him made me full of delirious sin
but that's because it was Love I was in.

Was it love I was in
or was I demented and hooked on lustful sin?
He never cared for me.
I was just a body he could use easily.
But I perpetuated the fraud.
I declared it was love I was in
and sure enough
since it looked soft and cushiony,
in, he let me fall.

I was in love just a few minutes gone by,
before the clouds cleared the noon day sky,
but this time as I heard his voice,
I felt the tears fill my eyes.
Cause love was out.
Where have I been
-acting stupid-
imaging it was love I was in?

I was in love in my previous life,
Then a man, I was married to a beautiful woman
who hated being my wife.
She took our children and sailed across the sea.
She said I was ugly, too ugly for others to see.
But I loved her still. Yes, I loved her more
because she was proud and dignified
and would not tolerate, even me,
after everything I did for her and my country,
would not tolerate me, valiant me
for an eyesore.

I was in love, teasing, frolicking from
his collapsible raft straight to my secluded cave.
His name was something like Mr. Majestic and
the world crowned him brave.
I pampered him day out and night in
but then he cried and sighed for his old life,
so I set him free, bound again to shipwreck
right back to his renowned strife.

I pray that the love I'm constantly in
is no consequential sin....
I am in love every time
I see an artist work, or a comic playfully lie.
I love heavyset women who sing the blues!
Don't you?
I love when fellas play ball, half nude.
I'm in love just about everyday
usually in some small, quirky way.

I was in love on the planet Zenex.
There everyone obeyed the law
"Pay Homage to Thine Sex".
Still I was too much for the populace
-alone or collectively-
for they decried my wanton taste.
So I left them: wobbling, exhausted and weak.

Now they regret having treated
their only sun, their source of life, like a freak.

I was in love the other day
Here on the juvenile earth.
Here, I let a mere modern-day human
expend me of my worth.
I let him dip into my treasures.
Let him row his boat down my rivers
'cause I wanted to be special, to be in,
so I alluded to the LOVE I was in.

Loss of Conviction

Hate to admit it.
I fell, I stumbled into the grave abyss.
I couldn't keep the torch lit.
I wasn't strong enough, I simply was not fit.
Not fit to carry the hopes and dreams
of those gone on.
I ran out of pep talk; steam.
Never knew how to toot my own horn.
I'm sorry but I'm gonna leave
it for the others to take up.
Of course it hurts, but I won't be a tease
pretending to drink while only sipping from the cup.
The cup of hope, dreams, work, success
that individuals pour, fill and drink-
so that the rest of the world may digest.
It crushes me... I can feel what you think.
You think I was gifted but ungrateful...
that I was strong, but grounded by lazy bones.
You think I'm abandoning a garden that's plentiful
instead to dwell in a yard full of stones.
I've delayed this departure long enough.
I've called and postponed, I've cancelled many times.
That's not true! That I'm leaving in a huff and a puff,
I'm going quietly, calmly; taking my turn in line.
The line of life – the line of reality.
where everyone keeps steady in place,
for only imagination and will allow for creativity.
In this line, I can look around and show my face.
Whereas before, I had to hide my true intentions
of mastering love, enjoying life and opening new dimensions.
Here, in my little human spot, there's simulated recreation.
Everything's mindless, devoid of mental stimulation.
Now I can get up and go to work
and just do what the master says.
No need to pretend to have ambition or lurk
in the trenches of the 'Just Approaching" promotion wedge.

Finally, when they ask me 'What's up?"
They won't be upset that I'm doing too much.
I've joined their team, and will drink from their victory cup.
I, too, have no plans, no dreams, no way to be touched.
The loss of conviction
at first weighs heavily on the human soul.
But then surely it must lighten
after all, the masses seem content without any goals.
I, me, I am goal-less now.
I have eternity to accept my position in this overcrowded
space.
Perhaps one day you'll pour one drop of your glory
down on my face in this parched, demented place.
Thank you for that. Have mercy on me.
I sinned against man, god and myself.
I Lost Conviction!
So turn and go fast and take heed for thyself!

Miss you
(Bebe Nymph)

On that morning
When she rushed away
When Atlas strong skies turned gray
When Poseidon's volcanoes sat in disarray
And suddenly Ogygia visibly vanished from the planet

All of us living there
We all landed in new places on the earth
To bring our gifts, our spirits of care
But remembered our simple island family, ever so gently.

We know, she had to go, to evolve, to experience herself
In her own way
Mama nymph, the mermen, me-Bebe Nymph and all who
once
Were comforted by her welcoming embrace
Will feel her once again,
When she returns and even if she transcends
Into that cosmic roaming ligament
We can't ever see
And like a capped bottle with a note inside
Babbling on the sea
It may take a while
But she'll get this note from me.

I miss you so, Calypso
Bebe Nymph

ULTIMATELY...

SPACE....Time...continuous...
Order,,,,CHAoS\\\\\\Malicious,
EVIL! Good.   Sacrilegious.

ultimately

You--Me--Delirious;
MAN: WOMAN: Nefarious!
black|||white|||congruous.

ultimately

joy/pain---Minds Rearranged.
Comfort/Displeasure///glass Stained?
Hope/MISERY.   Gravity-restrained.

ultimately

More Speed!   NO SPEED, please.
RED light**White Light**Cease!
No light.?.   Existence without fright?

ULTIMATELY...

World of Mine – Gaia!

Like the phoenix rising, flying high
your ancient maternal form weathers far flung miles
in order to replenish generations with generous
bounty
with all the necessities for my life sustaining energy!

Recollecting glances from the Apex of the Giza
pyramid
Another place where we once laughed and hid
I feel welcomed again to re-ascend
To this place that will always transcend

Any of my states of being
For my titan father is forever holding me ...up!

Bless you!
World of Mine,
Faithful Gaia!

Cosmic Cruise

{Gliding back in, into the earth's vibrations
I hear your songs, oh modern day Orpheus,
How lucky the capital region is
to have you – Deon CleanCutt!}

Your <u>Cosmic Cruise</u>
Is upsetting my orbital balance.
But when I splashed down,
It was <u>Tania's Bell</u> that you chimed
Forcing me to go pay
Overdue tribute to the <u>Pharoahs</u>.
But the massive drums
Led me astray,
dancing through your Dionysian <u>Summer Nights</u>.

Now, I'm left
On your bed, <u>Star Gazing</u>
professing 'Oh Orpheus Clean Cutt,
'<u>We need you!</u>'
How <u>Cleanly Fresh</u>
Are your strings tweaking
The peaking valleys
Of this new <u>World Stomp</u> view.

***Gallantly rescuing my stalked heart, inside the fort, poised
for the next victory...***

Your warrior essence could only be camouflaged, it never
recoiled into new skin
Hence, breathing in your "man-ness",
I could not help but to be infused with that warring fume
leaking from you.

How long could you dwell in real peace and abundant
happiness?
How long could you remain transfixed in bliss; kept from
bearing swords, armaments?
How could I envision even with all my sight
that you would turn on me, Battle ME? That you would seek
to dominate the one,
who you termed, your exclusive goddess of light?

Undaunted, I stood firm and remained undiminished
by your seething lust for totalitarianism.
Kudos - you did succeed in cracking the inner command post
of my cavernous fort,
tunneling through, you caused a rift to tear, forcing a chasm.

So do I bleed drips of sorrow?
Or do I shower droplets of freedom over the 'morrows'?

Do I hide away on a phantom island they'll never find?
Or do I disperse my love energy over the oceans,
across the streams, the squalls, the seas into the wilderness
of time?

I can't! Any longer retreat to a peripheral realm subject to
MT. Olympus' whims.
I have transcended all that mess and must meet the
requirements

of that orbital system, where I reside a satellite - the moon Calypso,
dancing around Saturn.   You see, life never dies – Cronus lives!

Gallantly my stalked heart is rescued! Grief-free!
For I knew love…yes that 'once upon a time' - where it blazed uninhibited in that everlasting, eternal moment so true.
Inside the fort of immortal life, I'll relive each eon of that moment, forever new.
I'll stand poised for the next victory, to champion those who choose to journey wherever love launches an odyssey.

I did it, though, I loved!   I LOVED you; even offered you immortality.
I know now, I love me and that I will always be.
I love LOVE. Love itself is the one, the only victory.
Honor Eros, for defeat is beat!

Joy in his HEART

Angel sent
Body lent, sweet fragrances, anointed scents.
Heaven graciously revealed this lovely creature.
Joyously here,
slightly aware of the value of her presence.

Clever and cute,
Pretty but smart.
Gentle, warm, astute...
The Joy in his HEART.

As morning arrives,
Everyone come alive, but only she makes him smile.
Nectar to taste, memories to erase, people to face...
Regardless of the pressure, she makes it ALL worthwhile.

Springtime refreshing,
Endearing as art,
Energy increasing!...
The Joy in his HEART.

Nighttime falls, couldn't do it all,
make note to stay away from family brawls.
So much weight to carry on his shoulders
Still every night, he summons her - the princess at the ball.

Sometimes silly,
But always willing to play the part.
Nothing is too 'kiddy'
for the Joy in his HEART.

Shamelessly he declares,
Quick to make you aware...
"She's my heart, my soul"
What sweeter words are there?

"She's my heart, my soul."
It's where he gets his start.
She's his baby, she's never too old
To be the Joy in his HEART.

I Digress...

My darling Calypso, I'm glad you did.
You didn't have to...
Of course, no one really has to do anything.
Somehow under the magnanimous lid
of the universe, order and chaos wrestle
forth the existence of glory, waste or sin.

I digress...

But you did.
I can devise no fancy way to say, I was touched-
so that my spine tingled, my mind ceased operations,
my soul felt the rush!
as it was lifted up in response to your loving nature.
You may say, it's because of your culture
that you act this way.
But I know it's not that simple,
for if it were,
I'd receive presents every living day.

I digress...

You, my dear are special, unique.
While you see the physical dimensions,
it's your internal senses that trigger your soul to seek
out the being within; once cleverly hidden beneath.
Not many seek to find
another's desire/
Society today forces us
to be selfish in our need to climb higher, higher...

I digress...

Thanks for emerging from amongst the masses
to share something of YOU
with someone who was merely passing

down one shaded avenue of your well-travelled life.
You gave freely, exercising your cosmic might
to demonstrate
the postulate
that little things aren't small along the spectrum of life.

I can digress no longer...

Your energy has enhanced my reality...
THANKS, my dear, for thinking of me.

(I recall this story you told me Odysseus and the silly song I made of it.)

HO HUM

Old ho hums,
reminiscing of the days
her guitar played their drums,
of how salty her dress misted
from the roving sailors come.
And it was not done,
they would smoke, eat till stuffed,
talk crazy stuff, drink heavily,
act up and frolic some mo,
all bless-ed night long.
Still those days are gone
and from her kitchen table
she hums her hymns, sacred songs
cause, today, life is…what it is….
…ho hum.

*(I loved this trip when we floated to that place that they shall
one day, call the U.S. Virgin Islands.)*

Josephine is her name.

*Josephine is her name.
She stuns you like Lady Holiday.
Not quite as outrageous as her namesake,
La Parisian, Josephine Baker.
NO! don't you approach her, the same
for you see, she's been anointed "Queen".
Men are quickly tamed for she executes fakers.*

*Josephine is her name
and does not simply imply, merely suggest,
instead "Josephine" radiantly manifests – Royalty.
And royalty marches on,
whether in the fiefdoms of Brooklyn,
or in the splendor of the Caribbean sun.
Her actions are too strong for mild terms like sin.*

*Josephine lives her name.
She carries trunks of jewels, clothes and shoes.
She's vocal! She's visual! She's regal!
Josephine lives fully, she need not impress you
but she does and you're consumed with it.
Her walk alone entraps men and diminishes women.
God rejoices in her – her voice, her presence, all too big –
perfectly fit.*

*Josephine is her name
and she won't be confined to your 'french' prison.
Her kiss erases all emotions you've ever known before.
She comes so that sensations transform into seasons
Poor Duke Clifford felt the sting of her lore.
Slaying the one whom objected that Josephine's name
was exclaimed at the impromptu moment.*

Or so the legend goes
for Josephine is her name
and many myths, realities convene to create, embellish
the story but the glory is hers alone.
No offspring can rise to the challenge
whether nurtured or nourished, too overpowered.
All planets to her spectacular sun, they cometh.

Josephine is her name.
Too beautiful in youth to be shy, embarrassed by it.
Too willful with age to succumb to it.
Look if you want with admiring eyes
as did the island governor or neon city hustlers.
Crave her desires for your own, if you wish.
Do you have that built in "Josephine" to deal with it?

Josephine transcends her name
whether you pronounce it with a European, New York or
Crucian accent.
She reads avidly, she sews...some say she prays
for the life we never knew she lived inside,
inside herself, her crowded apartment, her ancestral home.
They say while she was everyone's desire, she lived alone.

But Josephine is her name
so when you graced her palace with your entourage,
she served feasts surely prepared by chefs.
As fine garments laced her furniture, in her realm
a party materialized while your ego got massaged.
So you never wanted to leave
but like cancer under "chemo" pressure, you knew when to
get out!
Still your mental senses crave what you once devoured,
craving it still now, in your body throughout.

JOSEPHINE...Josephine is her name.

POETRY be mine

Poetry...
> Please be mine.
You've helped me throughout.
Brought me more comfort
than dancing, crying or wine.

Poetry...
> Thanks for relief
from the sorrows and miseries
and for helping me maintain some of my beliefs.

Poetry...
> I usually come to you
when I'm confused and YOU
always cheer me up when joy is long overdue.

Poetry...
> In you I can be me.
You listen, understand
and always say, "Be yourself, be free!"

Poetry...
> I praise you, say thank you
for everything you give, you've done,
as I usually do....flowing, through you.

Sung by Solomon

"Many waters can not quench love,
neither can the floods drown it."

Dearest Solomon,

Solomon, like every true muse, artist
    your songs, your psalms, your vibrations
        caress my stress, swelling back and
        forth over the ebbs of time.

Sitting here in my garden turned wilderness
    I feel your love akin to wind
        consoling me, for my love was merely
        pantomime.

How my soul hastens to absorb
    your manly pillars of strength,
        unafraid to raise the marbled towers of
        love, rightfully high!

Saffron, jewels, apples, spice, chains of gold,
    cedar and fir lined rooms, purple galore,
    chariots.
        No measure limited your willing ways
        to satisfy!

If only I were she or even one of the many
    whose garden you delighted in
        my flowers should bloom afresh, luring
        butterflies.

Had your locks held for me the drops of the night
    as your voice piped, "Beloved", my ravished
    heart
        would have known eternal delight 'til
        the day of man breaks.

Woman, as you are uniquely wise to know
unseals her fountain of love to pour forth
forevermore.
Just one man per generation
appreciates, that, its base shalln't
deface!

Alas, to sense your songs so beautiful and perfumed,
I fish them out of the pebbled quakes of time,
seasoning them like milk and honey
under my tongue; a keepsake.

Stirred up, I find, fresh, my cluster of grapes,
I behold my life, the lily amongst the thorns,
to rise now, to dance in the vineyards.
World, NEWSBREAK!

I wish every woman, a sage as beautiful and bold as
you -
sweet to the taste, to feed pomegranates,
embrace in a secret place.
Behold, gladness of heart is immortal,
once awake!

...and now RE-AWAKED!

Thank you,
Calypso

THE SENSE OF APPRECIATION

Beyond the screens of my imagination
are the windows of my knowledge.
Here, I find the sense of appreciation,
realizing, I am one of few with such a privilege.

Now's when I say THANK YOU
for everything I have and everything I've been given.
Because all my thoughts and feelings are true,
even though, from me, a lots been taken.

I do not like to see you cry,
I do not want to hear you complain!
Now you say that life seems weary,
But who's to blame?

I have the sense of appreciation
which I want to give to you.
You know there's no obligation,
But then,
Isn't it long overdue?

Tomorrow!

There's that pot of gold behind the shimmering rainbow
And nobody, but nobody can tell me "NO!"
For I know,
To each cloud there's more than a silver lining
And yours, and even mine, shall be shining
In that spectacular glow, we refer to as 'Tomorrow'.

Tomorrow is comprised of the enormity of the past,
Of today, the never was,
The words you forgot to say.
The dreams yearning to be
And man and woman and their immortality.

Tomorrow dwells not on yesterday
Nor does she cling to the merits achieved today
But rather sets out with a bang to overcome them all
As she proudly delights in having her own way.

I fear her not as I bid farewell to our yesterdays.
No, she doesn't promise your every dream to come true
But don't allow yourself to fear
The unchallenged. Forward March! Do something new!

THE TIME FOR ME

I know it is time
To live my life,
not just think about what I want;
To dream; to fantasize on and on.
But time to get up
and create the me
I envision me to be.

But
It's like I'm frozen in time,
Tied down by the old miseries,
The daily chore, the future anxieties of life.

I lack the energy
to jumpstart my battery
and that is the greatest worry of all.

So
NOW is the crucial,
The groundbreaking time!
This very instant
will convalesce into the remainder of my life.
Help me dear God, Creator of the universe.
Help me dear God, to locate the god within me.
Dear God, in unison, please help me
To finally BE all I can be.
All I want to be!
All in your sight that I must be.
You gave me my purpose and I've embraced the vision.
I choose to carry out my mission!!!

Please stop the slow decay of me.
Fill me again with your love and sanctifying grace
So I can clearly see
MYSELF IN TRUTH AND FOR DESTINY.
For the time was,

For the time is,
And perhaps for the last time
THE TIME SHALL BE
My time,
The time for me!

C'est la vie

C'est la vie. Oui, Oui.
Puissiez-vous etre heureux.
Vous etes libre.

TO MARKET I GO...
(Reap what you sow)

"You reap what you sow"
they lament, they chant over and over again.
I did, I tilled the soil, I chose the seeds,
poured jugs of water over fertile plain, rock, sand;
all-terrain.
I walked for miles roundabout in patches of garden,
I bent over, slipped, fell down,
pulled myself up, semi-propped;
so much work in the beginning.
I jerked up charming obnoxious weeds
so my plants could grow free.
I endured the elements and all the havoc
it brazenly wreaked upon me.
I shriveled like my crops some long days,
not sure how to reclaim my posture,
to stand up again, to indulge in the sun's rays.
I found myself cursing aloud; madly I complained.
Softly, I cried; forever I was afraid.
What if I harness all this labor
but I'm not right for market?
What if I make it to the trading place
but all my fruit and flowers are outright rejected?

What if...
What if I just do my endeavor best
And I'm pleased within\with my HARVEST?
What if I provide enough nourishment
to enrich my body, to stock bushels of encouragement?
What if I have enough
to save some aside
to give weary travelers in need,
to further their own lifelines.

To reap what I sow
takes countless decisions of what to grow.

Only at the feast (or the famine), will I know
what my harvest is worth; what I take in tow.

If I had to live forever, forever, forever!

If I had to live forever
> and see humans come and go
If I had to live forever
> through the springtime, through triggered snow,
If I had to live forever
> in the midst of this decadent space
If I had to live forever
> I would burn your triumphs into my soul's landscape.

If I had to live forever
> As I did; long, long before you came along.
If I had to live forever
> I would have lyrical Orpheus, compile me whispered
> songs.
If I had to live forever
> I would ask you, if you would care to join the
> assembly of gods.
If I had to live forever
> I would execute my divine rights to promote you from
mere king to eternal god.

If I had to live forever
> I would ask you about that, to see if you cared to
> further develop.
If I had to live forever
> I would have gladly step down my diva pride, to raise
> mortal you – UP!
If I had to live forever
> I would create more luscious figs and dates, and
> refresh your powers every day.
If I had to live forever
> I would shelter our requited love from their jealous,
> juvenile ways.

If I had to live forever

And the others of my calamitous clan laughed at me,
If I had to live forever
>*but, if you replied "yes", you yearned to share my*
>*immortality*
If I had to live forever
>*and you, thus declared, for me, your undivided love,*
If I had to live forever
>*I would take their rebuke and all the mockery they*
>*could think of.*

If I had to live forever
>*I would wish to spend my eternity with you,*
If I had to live forever
>*For as Cronos-Time has declared, 'Eternity, she must*
>*do'.*
If I had to live forever
>*Hence, once you said "no" to my humble offer*
If I had to live forever
>*I could then only remain upon the earth, through*
>*musical joy/blended laughter.*

If I had to live forever
>*I would disappear into the cosmos, beyond the*
>*heavens, to regenerate;*
If I had to live forever
>*I would require celestial cleansing, once you*
>*departed my gate.*
If I had to live forever
>*I would have self- destructed any physical remnants*
>*of my island or me.*
If I had to live forever
>*I would then return home to Gaia, only as a recurring*
>*memory upon the seas!*

If I had to live forever
>*I would not label my earthly stint as defeat,*
If I had to live forever

I would have been happy to fulfill any part of your
   odyssean destiny.
If I had to live forever
   I would praise the Fates and Graces to be part of the
   provocative show,
If I had to live forever
   I would rejoice to be eternal! To rhythmically be
   sung over and over again,
as Calypso!

If I had to live forever
   I could now dance happily as a wandering,
   masquerading gypsy
If I had to live forever
   gladly amused that those West Indians named their
   happy music like me.
If I had to live forever
   I'd be proud to share my namesake with these
   formerly enslaved masses,
If I had to live forever
   proud that on Atlas' first ocean, the colonial seas
   brewed SPIRIT into dam molasses.

If I had to live forever
   I would never again be that lonely island girl,
   isolated or doomed
If I had to live forever
   Instead I'd roamed from the Asteroid Belt to Saturn,
   often as a moon.
If I had to live forever
   I would travel like Orpheus or Apollo bringing
   musical notes to their ears,
If I had to live forever
   playing mass in their carnivals, rejoicing; reigning
   triumphs year after year,
a new Calypso!

If I had to live forever

I would keep that rotational season of love we shared
If I had to live forever
    Keep it like your composed but roaring confidence,
    showing no fear
If I had to live forever
    Keep it entwined with my blood and lymph nodes
If I had to live forever
    Always radiating its magnificent crystal powers
    throughout my now harmonious soul!

If I had to live forever...
    ...I would. Having experienced you, I would!
    For you were my destiny.
If I had to live forever
    ...Now returning to earth, and simultaneously
    rotating throughout the galaxies
If I had to live forever
    ...Being newborn into a life that is rhythmically free
    and set upon Atlas' sea
If I had to live forever
    ...Dancing to Orpheus' tortured melodies, being
    lyrically played for you and me.

If I had to live forever, having experienced You, I would!

If I had to live forever, forever, forever...

If I had to live forever, having experienced You, I would!
I would! I would

If I had to live forever, forever, forever...

    Forever.

Calypso,

Just know

*Your singing, your poetry captured
my soul.*

Odysseus

At Twilight ... Beautiful in My Sight

And the vacuous galaxy, mischievously hums....
"When we were beautiful for each other"
"When we were beautiful with each other"
"When we were beautiful because of each other"

Like erstwhile, sunken but clear gemstones
      Found deposited in muddy embankments
Disposed of without so much as an afterthought;
      Deep in winding tectonic fissures of rotating,
grinding plates,

Called forth by treacherous natural disasters
      That none of the mad scientists would dare claim,
Yet we knew because of the treachery of their laughter,
      They had dumped their exhaust and waste, upon us
      over and over again,
Across the waves of undulating, agitating centuries

And the tension filled galaxy, absurdly hums....
"When we were beautiful for each other"
"When we were beautiful with each other"
"When we were beautiful because of each other"

And while we cried out!
      Who cared if we were hurt?
We were just stones (ain't that strong?),
      Deep and useless in the dirt!
Somehow riding shotgun on a prison planet,
      They spun out into orbit, third one
Deep in; in a "Paradise"
      They crudely, dismissingly called Earth.
But there, everywhere, we washed up again and again
      And they ignored us, though fluorescent, yet again
Determining we had no significant value,
      But through our algorithm, we sang our song.
And as you gleamed in the sun for me,

I danced and winked in the moon for you!
So then we secretly, openly enjoyed
>   *the whispers of our secret symmetry in chants*
and our increasing excitement
>   *Forced our crusted layers to scream and rant.*
Til our encrusted shells begun to dissolve
>   *and the storytellers tripped themselves up about us*
>   *this time,*
And thus resolved to take us to their private storehouse and
>   *push us down*
>   *in the 'possibly-one-day-might-be-worth-something'*
>   *pile.*

And the self-serving galaxy, statistically hums....
"When we were beautiful for each other"
"When we were beautiful with each other"
"When we were beautiful because of each other"

But we churned about amongst tarred leaves as we
crystallized even more,
>   *Rejoicing that we were still together. Still*
>   *from the opening note of that one elliptical song,*
>   *Since that first day that the Universe minted us,*
>   *separately; jointly into existence.*
Hence, you were compellingly beautiful in my sight
>   *Leaving me 'enchanting' once and permanently,*
>   *reflected in your light.*
Invoking that they'll never fully expose us to their limited
vision
>   *of what is beauty and what is might!*
Let them wonder, extract, if we might be
>   *All that they have ever needed; yearned for?*
At this point, I no longer care,
>   *'cause being a remnant of your electromagnetic force*
>   *field is all I endeavor!*

And the replicating galaxy, characteristically hums....

"When we were beautiful for each other"
"When we were beautiful with each other"
"When we were beautiful because of each other"

With the approaching Dawn, they felt your pulsating,
reverberating strength;
      rescuing your potential from the recurring layers of
      heap;
Polishing you up to set you free onto the market shelves
where you
      Took that leap up into new spheres of influence.
Thus, I prayed they left you uncut as you were naturally
clean cut.
      I then dug in the trusted grind of dreamed-for Life,
The one, I once lived but not quite -
      as I finally took to heart the ancient lament that
'Da Dream' was meant to vanish in the ambiguity of the
Twilight!

And the greedy, insatiable galaxy, continually hums…
"When we were beautiful for each other"
"When we were beautiful with each other"
"When we were beautiful because of each other"…

With a new refrain

…I think I kept my part of
"Maybe we can inspire one another"
As I now return to before you….
To sun gazing on the meridian line of the forever never.

THE FORCE RETAINS THE POET AT HEART

The celestial hand holds all its poets, its heart.
Always yearning to fulfill its mission,
of turning the overlooked into art.
The heavens formed this compact from the start.
Prevailing upon certain men and women the urgings of the
pen,
irrevocably flowing through the currents in their hearts.
Not withstanding any and all other activity assigned in life,
caring less if allotted with farms, tools; husband or wife.
The poet at heart is compelled to answer the call,
to read the world the revelations of itself,
despite all its power and might.
The earthly trappings appear invisible.
Still, so many words, so many syllables
choke your insides, take over your being.
Your body and poetry become indivisible.
Seldom do you earn the equivalent of a meal.
Ultimately, it's futile – the pen, the brush, the voice shall not
yield!
Only the heavens sanction the oral, drawn or written
remarks.
Imagination meets the needs as words transform the deeds.
The force retains its flock, for you, the chosen are the poet at
heart.

Look around...See how far you have come!

Look how far you've come.
You took that special 'the time for me'
To accomplish your goals, to seek out your dreams!

Look how far you've come.
Whether you were supported or even if everyone turned
away,
you were sure to carry on and required yourself to dig deeper
anyway.

Look how far you've come.
To "market you go...reap what your sow"!
You did that while helping others; without letting your energy
slip low.

Look how far you've come.
Creating needed energy but not running anyone's else race,
Instead, using resilience and hardworking efforts to create
this new space.

Look how far you've come.
Turn around and look over your shoulder.
Wow, so many steps taken and even crushed some boulders!

Look how far you've come.
Say it loud...to yourself, not just a whisper, "I'm so proud of
you!"
Say it louder, in the mind and in the mirror, "I'm so proud of
you, too!"

Look how far you've come!
Take breaks. Rest when you're tired but keep striking!
Keep going! This is your journey! Keep Hiking!

Now look back, look around…and see how far you've come!
Look ahead and "Forward March!", because you are not
done.
Look around…Testify today to how far you have come!

Do it! Look around…See how far you have come!
Look how far you have come!
How far YOU have come!

Calypso ~ A Muse In!

When a muse is coined lustrous and one of a kind,
When carnivals come every year,
And are played from Greece, to lands still unknown, they'll
find
A breeze so powerful yet so free that bears
...a bursting name called Calypso,
... a muse dancing in your soul.

And she dances with you, because you want to dance
And she'll nourish you because your soul needs nurturing
too.
Then when you're spent and need an advance
Of supplies, she'll provide you with provisions and a canoe
...that's the nature of Calypso
...a muse comforting your soul.

History will twist and turn and bind
History will squeal, and pull and grind
Her name into a tug and war of captor or captive
But your mind will just want to recall all that felt so seductive
... in what your mind calls music – that's Calypso
...another part of your existence, a muse in your soul!

Calypso!

*Like music! She floats
across my emotions. Tides
surging – Calypso!*

Reference

Bennerson, Jo Anna. Greek Mythology Genealogy Chart and other charts, 2025

Canva, AI Images including infinity waves, 2025.

Hesiod. *Theogony*. Translated by Hugh G. Evelyn-White, Harvard University Press, 1914.

Homer. (1997). *The Odyssey* (Cyber Classics). Cyber Classics. ISBN 1-55701-203-2

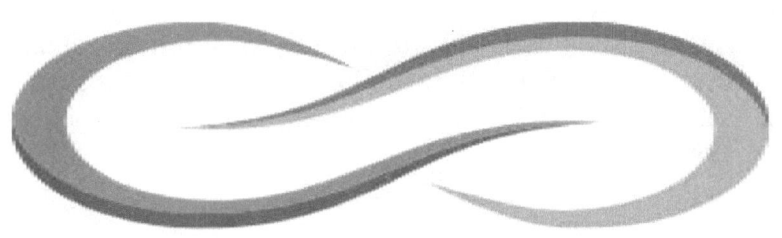

About the Author

Award winning inspirational author, visionary poet and transformational leader *Jo Anna Bella, Poet at Heart* (Dr. Poet) is the Goddess Poet, who is also known as Dr. Jo Anna Bennerson, PhD. Her writing encapsulates over thirty years of professional business management and information technology experience. She has a lifetime of community service, a love of poetry, with the research of Greek Mythology and ancient cultures to promote personal development, transformational leadership, as well as organizational alignment to facilitate break throughs and activate success.

Dr. Bennerson earned her PhD in 2021 focusing on leadership behaviors and succession management. She subsequently received an honorary PhD as well as the U.S. Presidential Lifetime Achievement Award for her far-reaching community service. An inspirational, motivational speaker, Dr. Bennerson has been certified by Les Brown's Legendary Speaker Academy in 2024. She is a coauthor of *The Motivation Manifesto: Les Brown's Principles for Inspired Living*. Her poem, **Forward March!** has been celebrated as an optimal motivational battle cry!

Dr. Jo Anna Bennerson's inspirational book, *Pinnacle Goddess Principles: Awakening and Unlocking Your Inner Power!- Red Star* initially earned three esteemed awards in 2024: the International Impact Award for Inspirational Writing, the LitPick 5-Star Book Review Award, and the Literary Titan Book Award. This powerful self-help guide weaves together Greek mythology, modern success stories, and actionable wisdom to empower readers on their journey to personal growth.

Jo Anna Bella, Poet at Heart reminds you that

*"Every decision you make is an action you take,
and every action you take is a decision you make!"*

FORWARD MARCH!

Thank you!

Forward March!

Jo Anna Bella,
Poet at Heart

www.ingramcontent.com/pod-product-compliance
Lightning Source LLC
Chambersburg PA
CBHW020601030726
47497CB00007B/2044